Sardar Hari Singh Nalwa

A Warrior who defeated Afghanistan, the country which was not defeated by USA and USSR

Ishwar Singh

pencil

ISBN 978-93-5667-956-6

Published in India 2023 by Pencil

A brand of
One Point Six Technologies Pvt. Ltd.
Unit no. 26, Ground Floor, Building A1,
Wadala Truck Terminal Road,
Near Post Office, Antop Hill, Mumbai - 400037
E connect@thepencilapp.com
W www.thepencilapp.com

Author biography

Ishwar Singh is a well-known and an internationally established author, whose books have been published more than 150 countries around the globe including USA, UK and Australia. He is an engineer, teacher, and public speaker. The author, a mechanical engineer by profession, has read and written poems, fiction, and research books for the past ten years. Additionally, the author is really interested in penning scholarly works on political and cultural science. Since he was 10 years old throughout his formative years, he has been a writer.

CONTENTS

Epigraph

"Amidst the turbulent landscape of empires and wars, one warrior stood out as a representation of resiliency, bravery, and unwavering will. The conqueror of Afghanistan, Sardar Hari Singh Nalwa, held firm in the face of forces that had baffled even the most powerful superpowers. His unflinching fortitude and steadfast spirit serve as a constant reminder that a warrior's ultimate power does not come from the number of his army but from the depth of his belief. This is the remarkable account of a warrior who made history by overcoming all obstacles and left an enduring imprint on the annals of battle."

Foreword

I have the utmost pleasure in introducing the outstanding book "Sardar Hari Singh Nalwa: A Warrior who Defeated Afghanistan, The Country Which Was Not Defeated by USA and USSR." The life, accomplishments, and historical importance of one of the most remarkable military commanders in Indian history are explored in this book.

Sardar Hari Singh Nalwa became a symbol of bravery, leadership, and tactical genius against the difficult geopolitical background of the 19th century. His military successes, especially his wins against the Afghan armies, not only helped to protect the Sikh Empire but also made a lasting impression on the history of the area.

We are led through Sardar Hari Singh Nalwa's trip by the author, who has done extensive study and has a thorough knowledge of the historical setting. We are transported to a time when political dominance was hotly fought and Afghanistan, a nation renowned for its tenacity, served as a dangerous foe to both the US and the USSR. However, Sardar Hari Singh Nalwa was the one who succeeded where others failed—an amazing achievement that says a lot about his military skill and strategic thinking.

This book is more than only a history. It explores the subtleties of conflict, the workings of power, and the unwavering spirit of a warrior who triumphed in the face of overwhelming challenges. We see the emergence of Sardar Hari Singh Nalwa within the Sikh Empire, his inventive military strategies, and his lasting influence in the fields of leadership, combat, and diplomacy via colorful descriptions and thorough research.

Each time we flip a page, we are taken back in time to a period when conflicts arose not only on the battlefield but also on the levels of philosophy, culture, and identity. We learn about the significant influence Sardar Hari Singh Nalwa had on Sikh nationalism, identity, and a community's collective consciousness.

This work is proof of the author's commitment to learning about the little-known facets of history. The author creates a vivid portrait of a warrior who not only protected his kingdom but also made a lasting impression on the history, culture, and art of battle of the area via engrossing storytelling and astute analysis.

I cordially encourage you to take this remarkable voyage via the pages of "Sardar Hari Singh Nalwa: A Warrior who Defeated Afghanistan, The Country Which Was Not Defeated by the USA and USSR." As you explore the life and legacy of a brilliant leader, be ready to be inspired, fascinated, and educated. May this book serve as an homage to Sardar Hari Singh Nalwa's unwavering spirit and inspire a fresh understanding of the bravery and sacrifices made by individuals who change the course of history.

Birinder Pal Kaur

Preface

There aren't many people in history who stand out as icons of bravery, valour, and military prowess. One such person whose astounding actions on the battlefield have forever altered the course of history is Sardar Hari Singh Nalwa. Nalwa, a fighter of outstanding talent who was born during the turbulent Sikh Empire, came to notoriety by leading his armies to victories that would be considered as amazing even in the face of terrible foes.

When we take into account the circumstances of Sardar Hari Singh Nalwa's period, the importance of his accomplishments becomes even more obvious. Afghanistan, a nation renowned for defying foreign invasions, has historically resisted the power of empires such as the British Empire, the Soviet Union, and the United States. Nevertheless, it was Nalwa who, despite all difficulties, was able to subdue Afghan warriors and extend the Sikh Empire's boundaries into Afghan territory.

This book, "Sardar Hari Singh Nalwa: A Warrior who Defeated Afghanistan, the Country which was not Defeated by USA and USSR," explores the incredible life and military battles of this exceptional commander. It tries to solve the mystery surrounding Nalwa by illuminating his tactical vision, creative approach, and unflinching resolve in the face of difficulty.

We seek to offer a thorough narrative of Nalwa's journey, from his rise to prominence in the Sikh Empire to his epic battles against Afghan armies, by rigorous study and examination of historical sources. We examine the geopolitical environment of the era, Afghanistan's historical backdrop, and the political climate of the 19th century. We may understand the scope of Nalwa's accomplishments by looking at the significant wars and invasions that Afghanistan has experienced.

We also look at Nalwa's tactical prowess, leadership traits, preparations, and defensive tactics—all of which were crucial in helping him defeat strong foes. We also explore his work as the governor of Peshawar, where he implemented reforms, built infrastructure, and encouraged trade and commerce, all of which had a long-lasting effect on the area.

The extension of the Sikh Empire into Afghan territory is also examined in this book, along with Nalwa's diplomacy and talks with Afghan authorities, as well as the shifting dynamics and tensions between the two powers. We examine Nalwa's methods' ongoing effect, his impact on the geopolitical environment, and his historical importance in Indian and Afghan history.

In addition to paying honor to Sardar Hari Singh Nalwa's exceptional life and achievements, we hope that this book will help readers get a greater knowledge of the historical background, military tactics, and cultural relevance of his legacy. Through these pages, we want to uplift readers with the tale of a real warrior—a leader whose unshakeable spirit and resolve endured the test of time.

Join us on this exploration and learning adventure as we learn about the incredible life of Sardar Hari Singh Nalwa, a warrior who overcame adversity and left a lasting impact in history.

Ishwar Singh

Acknowledgements

To my parents, Sardar Pal Singh and Sardarni Amarjit Kaur, I would like to express my sincere gratitude and appreciation for their unwavering support and encouragement throughout the writing of this book, "Sardar Hari Singh Nalwa: A Warrior who Defeated Afghanistan, The Country which was Not Defeated by USA and USSR."

This book would not exist without their support, advice, and faith in my ability. They have always been my pillars of support, giving me the drive and inspiration I need to pursue my love of books and history.

They went beyond simple encouragement in their constant support. They devoted a lot of time to sharing their information, opinions, and life stories, which enriched the book's richness and authenticity. Their significant contributions have given the story depth and perspective, enabling a thorough examination of Sardar Hari Singh Nalwa's life and accomplishments.

I also want to thank them for their unfailing patience during the endless hours of research, writing, and revision. Their patience and encouragement during the difficult process of authoring this book have served as a continual source of inspiration and confidence.

I consider myself very fortunate to have such amazing parents who have always fostered my intellectual curiosity and instilled in me a profound respect for our cultural history. My own love of history and storytelling has been greatly influenced by their dedication to preserving our past and developing a feeling of pride in our heritage.

I want to close by sincerely thanking Sardar Pal Singh and Sardarni Amarjit Kaur for their support, affection, and important contributions to this work. This project has only been made possible because of their unshakable faith in me and their steadfast affection. I give them my thanks and appreciation by dedicating this book to them.

Sardar Hari Singh Nalwa

Chapter 1

Introduction to Sardar Hari Singh Nalwa

1.1 Early life and background

In Gujranwala, Punjab, which was then a part of the Sikh Empire, Sardar Hari Singh Nalwa was born in 1791. He is a significant person in Sikh history. He came from a prestigious family of the Sandhawalia clan, which was renowned for its military skill and devotion to the cause of the Sikhs. Gurdial Singh, Nalwa's father, was a reputable commander in the Sikh army, and this family ties to the armed forces would influence Nalwa's future.

Nalwa showed extraordinary physical prowess and martial talent at a young age. His early education was provided by Sikh experts, who taught him Sikh philosophy, literature, and military tactics. Nalwa absorbed a strong sense of integrity, discipline, and dedication to his religion from his father and other notable Sikh elders.

Growing up at a time of political unrest, the young Nalwa saw the wars and power plays that afflicted Punjab. Following the fall of the Mughal Empire, the area was plunged into a power vacuum, with competing Afghan and Sikh tribes contending for dominance. Nalwa's perspective would be shaped by these trying times, which also gave him important insights into the workings of power and conflict.

Nalwa's fighting skill and innate leadership skills were rapidly acknowledged by the Sikh community. He took part in his first military operation at the juvenile age of 17 under Maharaja Ranjit Singh, the charismatic commander who sought to bring the Sikh misls (confederacies) together into a potent kingdom. Throughout this war, Nalwa's courage and strategic prowess were on display, gaining acclaim and admiration from his allies and superiors.

Nalwa's reputation as a fearsome warrior increased with each succeeding military operation. He had extraordinary proficiency with a variety of weapons, including swords, spears, and guns. The nickname "Fateh Dost," which translates to "the victorious friend," was given to him after a streak of triumphs that were made possible by his physical prowess, agility, and tactical acumen.

Along with his military skill, Nalwa's ascent to popularity was also credited to his steadfast devotion to Maharaja Ranjit Singh. He became close to the Maharaja, who trusted him with significant duties after recognizing his ability. The two leaders' excellent collaboration was made possible by their mutual trust and friendship.

The early years of a great warrior may be seen in Sardar Hari Singh Nalwa's life and background. The unstable political climate of Punjab influenced every step of Nalwa's career, from his early encounters on the battlefield to his upbringing in a family with a strong military lineage. His great abilities and unshakable commitment to the Sikh cause laid the foundation for his outstanding accomplishments in the years to come.

In Gujranwala, Punjab, which was then a part of the Sikh Empire, Sardar Hari Singh Nalwa was born in 1791. He is a significant person in Sikh history. He came from a prestigious family of the Sandhawalia clan, which was renowned for its military skill and devotion to the cause of the Sikhs. Gurdial Singh, Nalwa's father, was a reputable commander in the Sikh army, and this family ties to the armed forces would influence Nalwa's future.

Nalwa showed extraordinary physical prowess and martial talent at a young age. His early education was provided by Sikh experts, who taught him Sikh philosophy, literature, and military tactics. Nalwa absorbed a strong sense of integrity, discipline, and dedication to his religion from his father and other notable Sikh elders.

Growing up at a time of political unrest, the young Nalwa saw the wars and power plays that afflicted Punjab. Following the fall of the Mughal Empire, the area was plunged into a power vacuum, with competing Afghan and Sikh tribes contending for dominance. Nalwa's perspective would be shaped by these trying times, which also gave him important insights into the workings of power and conflict.

Nalwa's fighting skill and innate leadership skills were rapidly acknowledged by the Sikh community. He took part in his first military operation at the juvenile age of 17 under Maharaja Ranjit Singh, the charismatic commander who sought to bring the Sikh misls (confederacies) together into a potent kingdom. Throughout this war, Nalwa's courage and strategic prowess were on display, gaining acclaim and admiration from his allies and superiors.

Nalwa's reputation as a fearsome warrior increased with each succeeding military operation. He had extraordinary proficiency with a variety of weapons, including swords, spears, and guns. The nickname "Fateh Dost," which translates to "the victorious friend," was given to him after a streak of triumphs that were made possible by his physical prowess, agility, and tactical acumen.

Along with his military skill, Nalwa's ascent to popularity was also credited to his steadfast devotion to Maharaja Ranjit Singh. He became close to the Maharaja, who trusted him with significant duties after recognizing his ability. The two leaders' excellent collaboration was made possible by their mutual trust and friendship.

The early years of a great warrior may be seen in Sardar Hari Singh Nalwa's life and background. The unstable political climate of Punjab influenced every step of Nalwa's career, from his early encounters on the battlefield to his upbringing in a family with a strong military lineage. His great abilities and unshakable commitment to the Sikh cause laid the foundation for his outstanding accomplishments in the years to come.

1.2 Rise to prominence in the Sikh Empire

His outstanding military prowess, unshakable devotion, and strategic insight all contributed to Hari Singh Nalwa's ascent to prominence in the Sikh Empire. Nalwa was gifted in the martial arts from an early age. Nalwa was given leadership of the Khalsa Army by Maharaja Ranjit Singh, the creator of the Sikh Empire, because of his ability.

Nalwa advanced through the ranks under the direction of Maharaja Ranjit Singh and developed a reputation as a brave and talented fighter. He took part in a number of military operations while exhibiting extraordinary courage and tactical acumen. Nalwa won the respect and affection of his superiors and other troops as a result of his victories on the battlefield.

Nalwa's ability to lead was put to the test when he was chosen to serve as the governor of Peshawar, an important border province. In this capacity, he not only protected the Sikh Empire's borders but also led a number of military campaigns to increase the empire's power. Nalwa's strategic insight and managerial prowess were instrumental in strengthening Sikh dominance over the area.

The fact that Nalwa was able to repel successive Afghan assaults is one of his most illustrious accomplishments. Afghanistan presented a serious obstacle for foreign powers because of its imposing reputation as an unconquerable country. Nalwa was able to resist Afghan raids and protect the Sikh Empire's boundaries because to his superior military skills and in-depth understanding of the region.

Nalwa's military expertise extended beyond just defensive tactics. He oversaw many military operations that expanded the Sikh Empire's borders into Afghani territory. His triumphs in locations like Jamrud, Multan, and Kashmir served as evidence of his capacity to organize and carry out intricate military operations.

Along with his military successes, Nalwa was also very important to the management and government of the Sikh Empire. He carried out a number of reforms, upgraded the country's infrastructure, and encouraged business and trade. The Sikh Empire's border territories were made stable and prosperous thanks in large part to Nalwa's administrative skills.

Hari Singh Nalwa became one of the most well-known and significant individuals in the Sikh Empire because to his unshakable commitment, outstanding military prowess, and administrative nous. His ascent to fame was evidence of his commitment, bravery, and leadership skills. Because of his extraordinary accomplishments, Nalwa has become a legendary character in Sikh history.

1.3 Overview of the geopolitical context in the region

It is crucial to take into account the geopolitical environment of the area at the time in order to comprehend the importance of Hari Singh Nalwa's triumphs and his contribution to the Sikh Empire's wars with Afghanistan.

Early in the 19th century, the area bordering Afghanistan saw a complicated and unstable political environment. Multiple regional powers competed for control of different regions as a result of the power vacuum left by the waning Mughal Empire. Maharaja Ranjit Singh oversaw the Sikh Empire, which grew to be a powerful force in Punjab and aimed to spread its authority.

Afghanistan was experiencing internal unrest at the same time due to conflicting groups and tribal conflicts. An ununified Afghan state resulted after the demise of the Ahmad Shah Durrani-founded Durrani Empire. Afghanistan became a desirable target for neighboring nations, especially the Sikh Empire, because to this power vacuum.

The Great Game, a geopolitical war between the Russian and British Empires for control of Central Asia, may also be used to understand the Afghan-Sikh clashes. As part of their geopolitical goals, both countries attempted to forge alliances and install benevolent governments in Afghanistan and its surrounding territories.

In light of this, Hari Singh Nalwa's successes against the Afghan army had a significant impact. The resilient Afghanistan, often known as the "Graveyard of Empires," had established itself as a formidable foe for foreign forces, especially the British and Russians. The Sikh Empire did, however, manage to secure important victories over the Afghan troops because to Nalwa's military acumen and strategic ingenuity, which further cemented the Sikh Empire's grip in the area.

In addition to securing the Sikh Empire's frontiers, Nalwa's conquests allowed it to extend its sphere of influence into Afghan-controlled areas. This had a significant impact on the balance of power in the area since it put the Afghan government to the test and increased the Sikh Empire's influence outside of Punjab.

Furthermore, the Sikh Empire's effective defense of Nalwa against Afghan incursions demonstrated its military might and emphasized its potential as a regional force. It established the Sikh Empire as a major player in the wider geopolitical scene and showed off the might and tenacity of the Sikh soldiers.

Overall, Hari Singh Nalwa's reign saw a geopolitical situation in the area that was marked by changing power relations, rivalry between regional powers, and the greater framework of the Great Game. The Sikh Empire's boundaries were secured by Nalwa's triumphs over Afghanistan, which also had a lasting effect on the balance of power in the area and how the Sikh Empire was seen as a major role there.

Chapter 2

The Afghan Kingdom and its Challenges

2.1 Historical background of Afghanistan

Afghanistan has a long and varied past that has affected its culture, politics, and identity. This history is rich and complicated. The area has been inhabited since prehistoric times and has seen the rise and fall of countless civilizations. It is located at the crossroads of Central Asia.

The Indus Valley Civilization, which lived approximately 2500 BCE, was one of the first civilizations in Afghanistan that is known to have existed. Later, the Achaemenids, Greeks, Mauryans, and Kushans, among other empires and dynasties, had an impact on the area. The cultural and architectural legacy of the area was profoundly influenced by these influences.

Islam was brought to Afghanistan in the seventh century CE, ushering in a profound change in the region's religious and cultural environment. Afghanistan developed into a significant hub of Islamic civilisation, with well-known towns like Herat, Ghazni, and Balkh acting as educational and commercial hubs along the Silk Road.

Afghanistan has had multiple foreign invasions and conquests throughout its history. Examples include the

Arab conquest in the 7th and 8th centuries, the Mongol invasion in the 13th century, and the dominance of the Timurid Empire in the 14th and 15th centuries. As a consequence of these invasions, indigenous customs often mixed with those of the conquerors, adding to Afghanistan's rich cultural mosaic.

Afghanistan developed into a coherent state in the 18th and 19th centuries under the rule of many Pashtun dynasties, notably the Durrani Empire established by Ahmad Shah Durrani. The empire expanded its dominion and authority over a large portion of modern-day Pakistan and Afghanistan.

Afghanistan served as a theater of conflict for conflicts between European nations during the Great Game in the 19th century. To protect their imperial interests in Central Asia, the British and Russian Empires strove to acquire influence and authority in Afghanistan. The internal dynamics of Afghanistan were further exacerbated by this geopolitical strife, which also fueled times of unrest.

Afghanistan had substantial political and socioeconomic changes throughout the 20th century. In 1919, the nation gained its freedom from British colonial domination, creating a monarchy that lasted until the 1970s. Following the monarchy's reign, there were many coups, political upheavals, and the final ascent of the communist regime, supported by the Soviet Union, in 1978.

A significant turning point in Afghanistan's history occurred with the Soviet Union's invasion in 1979. Massive human misery and destruction were the outcome of the ensuing ten-year battle between the Soviet troops and

Afghan resistance organizations, known as the Mujahideen.

Afghanistan saw civil war in the 1990s, and the Taliban, an Islamist extremist organization, rose to power and took over Kabul as the country's capital in 1996. International criticism of the Taliban's repressive rule and its protection of foreign terrorists—most notably Osama bin Laden—led to the US-led invasion of Afghanistan in 2001.

Afghanistan has since had a difficult transition to a stable and democratic government. But the nation still has to deal with persistent issues including political instability, security worries, racial tensions, and socioeconomic advancement.

Understanding the intricacies and forces that have produced Afghanistan's current difficulties and ambitions requires an understanding of the country's historical history. It offers insightful information about the rich cultural legacy, geopolitical conflicts, and tenacity of its people throughout the ages.

2.2 Political landscape during the 19th century

Afghanistan and the surrounding area saw a dynamic and changeable political environment throughout the 19th century. Multiple Pashtun dynasties governed Afghanistan, and internal conflicts, invasions, and territorial disputes all had an impact on the country's political development.

Ahmad Shah Durrani, who in the middle of the 18th century formed the current state of Afghanistan, was one of the most prominent individuals during this time. His dominion, sometimes known as the Afghan dominion or the Durrani Empire, included a sizable section of modern-day Pakistan and Afghanistan. Tribal strife and the region's mixed ethnic population made it difficult for the empire to establish centralized rule.

The conflict between regional powers and the presence of outside forces further complicated Afghanistan's political environment. As part of the "Great Game," the British and Russian Empires strove to increase their strategic and political might in the area, including Afghanistan. This geopolitical competition increased tensions and made Afghanistan more open to foreign invasion.

Afghanistan saw a number of invasions and battles during the 19th century that put its political stability to the test. The Anglo-Afghan Wars, fought between Afghanistan and the British Empire, were important occasions that altered the political environment. In the course of the First Anglo-Afghan War (1839–1842), British forces were massacred as they withdrew from Kabul. Although the British won the Second Anglo-Afghan War (1878–1880), Afghanistan kept its independence and only allowed a little amount of British involvement over its internal affairs.

The political environment of Afghanistan was significantly shaped by internal power struggles as well. Periods of instability and changing alliances resulted from conflicts between various Pashtun clans and groups fighting for the crown. For instance, the competition between the Durrani dynasty's Barakzai and Sadozai lineages led to political strife and power battles that had an effect on Afghanistan's government.

Another important component of the political scene in the 19th century was territorial disputes and wars with neighboring powers. Afghanistan and the Sikh Empire, ruled by Maharaja Ranjit Singh, fought one other for possession of lands in modern-day Pakistan. Borders shifted as a consequence of the Sikh-Afghan battles, and there was a push-and-pull relationship between the two nations.

Overall, internal power struggles, foreign interventions, and territorial conflicts dominated Afghanistan's political environment throughout the 19th century. Geographically, ethnically, and strategically, the nation became a focus of both regional and global affairs. The difficulties and complexity Afghanistan would continue to encounter in the years to come were set in motion by these political forces.

2.3 Major conflicts and invasions faced by Afghanistan

Afghanistan has endured several wars and invasions throughout its history, primarily as a result of its advantageous position at the crossroads of Central Asia. Throughout history, numerous regional and international countries have vied for control of it because of its hilly geography, ethnic variety, and geopolitical significance. Afghanistan has had significant wars and invasions that have influenced its history and had a long-lasting effect on its people from antiquity to the present.

Alexander the Great's invasion of Afghanistan in the fourth century BCE is one of the oldest documented incursions into the country. The indigenous tribes and kingdoms fiercely resisted the Macedonian conqueror's attempts to expand his power eastward. Despite difficulties, Alexander was able to take over sections of Afghanistan, establishing a lasting Greek impact on the people and architecture of the area.

Afghanistan became a battlefield for numerous regional powers in the centuries that followed. Islam was introduced to the area via Arab invasion in the seventh and eighth century, which resulted in the foundation of a Muslim state. Afghanistan also saw Mongol invasions in the 13th century, which caused extensive damage and the dissolution of earlier power systems.

The Mughal Empire, which had its headquarters in India, attempted to expand its dominance into Afghanistan throughout the 16th century. The Mughal dynasty's first ruler, Emperor Babur, conquered Afghanistan and established rule over part of the country. However, local Pashtun tribes resisted the Mughals, and their control over Afghanistan remained shaky.

Afghanistan saw invasions and wars with nearby nations in the 18th and 19th centuries, particularly the Persian and Sikh Empires. A number of battles and territorial conflicts resulted from the Persian Empire's attempts, under different dynasties, to impose its authority over Afghanistan. Throughout this time, the Afghan-Persian hostilities persisted sporadically, with changing boundaries and shifting power structures.

The Sikh-Afghan Wars were another important struggle that influenced Afghanistan's history. Under Maharaja Ranjit Singh, the Sikh Empire tried to expand its borders and fought Afghanistan for control of important areas like Peshawar and Kashmir. Back-and-forth fighting occurred throughout these wars, with both sides claiming triumphs and incurring casualties. In the end, the Sikh Empire's rule over these areas was transient since Afghanistan was able to drive back Sikh armies and recover control.

The so-called "Great Game" in Afghanistan during the 19th century also saw the participation of foreign powers, particularly the British and Russian Empires. By establishing Afghanistan as a buffer state against Russian incursion into South Asia, the British intended to halt this development. As a result, there were political interference in Afghan issues as well as diplomatic hedging and strategic alliances.

A significant war, the First Anglo-Afghan War (1839–1842), was the outcome of British efforts to seize control of Afghanistan. Shah Shuja, a puppet monarch that the British imposed, was met with fierce opposition from Afghan tribes and religious authorities. Few survivors made it back to British India as the war came to a conclusion with a devastating British withdrawal from Kabul.

Another notable battle was the Second Anglo-Afghan War (1878–1880), which the British started in an effort to offset what they saw as Russian hegemony in Afghanistan. Invading British soldiers removed Yakub Khan's government and replaced it with one that was more kind. But as a result of broad opposition to the war, Afghan soldiers started a fruitful guerrilla fight against the British. The Treaty of Gandamak, which secured Afghan independence but gave the British extensive authority over Afghan affairs, put an end to the war.

Early in the 20th century, Afghanistan had more wars and invasions. Political turmoil, including internal power struggles and coups d'état, occurred throughout the nation. An important turning point was reached when Afghanistan successfully reclaimed its complete independence from British rule during the Third Anglo-Afghan War of 1919.

Afghanistan got involved in the Cold War conflicts between the United States and the Soviet Union in the second part of the 20th century. It was a significant event when the Soviet Union invaded Afghanistan in 1979, and it had far-reaching effects. The Soviets' attempt to maintain a communist government resulted in a 10-year war with Afghan opposition organizations known as the Mujahideen. The Afghan people were caught in the crossfire between Soviet troops and the Mujahideen, who had assistance from the United States and other nations, causing the conflict to cause great human misery. The battle also witnessed the rise of extremist organizations like the Taliban that would eventually influence Afghanistan's destiny.

Afghanistan entered a bloody civil war in 1989, after the Soviet departure. As several warlords and groups fought for control, there was intense bloodshed all around. In 1996, a harsh government was installed in Kabul thanks to the Taliban, an Islamist extremist organisation. Brutal persecution, a rigid application of Islamic law, and the protection of foreign terrorists—most notably Osama bin Laden and Al-Qaeda—were characteristics of their regime.

With the American-led invasion in 2001, Afghanistan entered a new era of strife. Operation Enduring Freedom was started by the US after the 9/11 terrorist attacks in order to overthrow the Taliban and destroy Al-Qaeda. The Taliban administration was overthrown by the invasion, and a new government was installed in Afghanistan.

Despite early victories, the battle eventually turned into a prolonged insurgency as the Taliban regained power and waged a persistent insurgency against Afghan and foreign troops. Significant numbers of people have been killed, displaced, and the nation continues to be unstable as a consequence of the conflict.

Major wars and invasions have left their marks on Afghanistan's political, social, and cultural environment throughout its history. The Afghan people's fortitude and tenacity have often been put to the test as they deal with the difficulties brought on by internal power struggles, rivalries in the area, and foreign invasions. The nation is still working to achieve stability, peace, and its long-term goals of prosperity.

Chapter 3

Hari Singh Nalwa's Military Genius

3.1 Leadership qualities and strategic vision

Sardar Hari Singh Nalwa was a brilliant leader with outstanding leadership skills and a clear strategic vision, all of which were crucial to his success. He was a respected figure in the Sikh Empire and a fearsome foe for the Afghan army because to his military prowess and leadership abilities.

Hari Singh Nalwa was known for his unrelenting tenacity and fearlessness in the face of adversity, which was one of his most important leadership traits. He commanded his forces from the front lines, constantly displaying courage and motivating his men to fight valiantly. Nalwa's courage inspired his soldiers with confidence and a strong feeling of brotherhood, which in turn cultivated a strong sense of devotion and dedication.

Nalwa was well-known for his keen military judgment and foresight. He was quite knowledgeable about the terrain and the value of fortifications in battle. He was able to successfully defend his holdings and mount successful offensives against the Afghan troops because to his ability to plot and adjust to changing circumstances. Nalwa's strategic insight allowed him to outwit his foes and win significant triumphs for the Sikh Empire.

His excellent sense of organization and discipline was another important aspect of Nalwa's leadership. He saw keeping a well-organized, disciplined army as essential to the accomplishment of his military operations. Nalwa placed a strong emphasis on his soldiers' thorough training, efficient command systems, and open lines of communication. This methodical technique promoted unity and made sure that his men were ready for combat and willing to fight.

Nalwa was renowned for his ability to form coalitions and for his diplomatic prowess. To enhance the Sikh Empire's position and fend off foreign challenges, he understood the need of forming strategic alliances with local rulers. Nalwa forged connections with tribes and municipal authorities via diplomatic dialogues and cunning diplomacy, winning their support and cooperation. These partnerships were essential to safeguarding his holdings and growing the Sikh Empire's sphere of influence.

Nalwa was a commander who cared greatly about the wellbeing of his soldiers and the people he was in charge of. He was concerned about the wellbeing of his troops and made steps to secure it by giving them the right food, access to medical treatment, and financial assistance, among other things. Nalwa's care for his soldiers' well-being not only encouraged loyalty, but also forged a solid relationship of trust between him and them.

Nalwa has a remarkable attention to detail and organizing abilities. He devoted great attention to supply chains, resource management, and logistics, all of which were essential for conducting effective military operations. His careful preparation and logistical know-how made sure that his men had the right tools and assistance in the field.

Additionally, Nalwa was a forward-thinking leader who recognized the value of infrastructure and development for the continuity and expansion of his territory. He started a number of infrastructural initiatives, including as the building of forts, roads, and irrigation systems, all of which enhanced both the lifestyles of the populace and the defense of his territory. The areas he controlled had a lasting effect from Nalwa's vision for development, which contributed to their long-term success.

Sardar Hari Singh Nalwa stood out as a unique leader due to his extraordinary leadership abilities and strategic vision. His exploits and wins were made possible by his boldness, military prowess, strategic thought, discipline, diplomatic abilities, and care for the welfare of his soldiers. The Sikh Empire's frontiers were secured, its power was increased, and Nalwa became a respected character in the history of the area thanks to his leadership.

3.2 Organization and modernization of the Sikh Army

Under Sardar Hari Singh Nalwa's direction, the Sikh Army was organized and modernized, which significantly changed the Sikh Empire's military might. Nalwa was instrumental in restructuring and bolstering the army, bringing forth changes that improved its efficiency and allowed the Sikh Empire to defend its realms and increase its power.

The creation of a clear command structure was one of the key components of the Sikh Army's organizational structure. Nalwa put in place a hierarchical structure that established distinct lines of authority and guaranteed effective coordination and communication between various groups. This command organization allowed for quick decisions, efficient unit deployment, and coordinated actions on the battlefield.

Nalwa understood the value of training and discipline in forging a powerful combat force. He placed a strong emphasis on his troops completing demanding training regimens that focused on physical fitness, weapon competence, and tactical abilities. To improve the forces' preparation for battle, regular drills and exercises were carried out. The Sikh Army was made to seem professional and cohesive by the focus placed on training and discipline.

Nalwa offered advancements in armament and military technology to upgrade the Sikh Army. He made sure that his forces had the most modern equipment available at the time because he understood the importance of modern guns and artillery in battle. Nalwa promoted the production and procurement of contemporary weapons, cannons, and other artillery pieces, greatly enhancing the Sikh Army's ability to fire.

Nalwa recognized the importance of logistics and supply management in maintaining military operations and devoted attention to it. To guarantee a consistent supply of necessities like food, ammunition, and medical supplies, he set up effective supply systems. This emphasis on logistics improved the Sikh Army's mobility and stamina, allowing it to function well in a variety of terrains and difficult circumstances.

The building of fortifications and defensive constructions was a crucial component of the Sikh Army's development. Nalwa started building a number of forts and fortified outposts that were strategically placed around the Sikh Empire's frontiers. These forts supplied the Sikh Army with a safe operating base and acted as defensive strongholds. They served to prevent enemy incursions and to support the maintenance of territorial sovereignty.

Nalwa introduced administrative changes in addition to organizational and technology upgrades to improve the efficiency of the Sikh Army. He set up procedures for hiring, paying, promoting, and rewarding employees, assuring accountability and fairness throughout the military ranks. The administrative changes made by Nalwa raised military morale, rewarded achievement, and instilled a feeling of professionalism.

Under Nalwa's direction, the Sikh Army's modernization efforts greatly improved both its offensive and defensive capability. Nalwa's reforms made sure that the military was modern, disciplined, and well-organized so that it could counter challenges from outside and maintain internal stability. During a time of geopolitical obstacles and wars, these activities were very important in preserving the Sikh Empire's lands and growing its power.

Overall, Sardar Hari Singh Nalwa's organization and modernisation of the Sikh Army were crucial in making it into a powerful military force. His focus on discipline, training, equipment, logistics, fortifications, and administration led to the development of a well-organized and effective military army that could fend off outside attack and defend the Sikh Empire's interests. The Sikh Empire's military might was improved by Nalwa's reforms, which also helped the empire gain notoriety at the period.

3.3 Nalwa's innovative tactics and military achievements

His military prowess and reputation for creative thinking contributed significantly to Sardar Hari Singh Nalwa's victories on the battlefield. He stood out as a superb military commander due to his strategic thinking, versatility, and capacity to take advantage of his enemies' vulnerabilities.

Guerrilla warfare strategies were one of Nalwa's most important inventions. He expertly used hit-and-run strategies, ambushes, and surprise assaults against his adversaries because of his understanding of the geography of the area. Nalwa successfully cut off enemy supply lines, caused fatalities, and demoralized his adversaries by making use of Afghanistan's hilly terrain and the Northwest Frontier Province. By using these guerilla strategies to defeat stronger, more conventional armies, Nalwa was able to make the most of his few resources.

Nalwa also showed a great comprehension of the value of defenses and fortifications. He built and reinforced a large number of forts, including the well-known Jamrud Fort, which were strategically placed to control important trade routes and protect crucial territory. These forts offered safe grounds for starting offensive operations in addition to acting as defensive bastions. Because of Nalwa's expertise in defensive tactics and construction, his forces were able to successfully stave off enemy assaults and endure protracted sieges.

Nalwa was an exceptional offensive strategist in addition to his defensive abilities. In combat, he used creative tactics that often caught his opponents off surprise. One such instance was Nalwa's brave night assault on the Afghan soldiers at the Battle of Shopian in 1819. Nalwa successfully confused the opposition and suffered significant casualties by striking unexpectedly during the night, leading to a resounding win. This displayed his capacity for original thought and the use of non-traditional strategies to advance on the battlefield.

The military prowess of Nalwa went beyond the use of defensive and offensive tactics. Through clever annexations and alliances, he played a key role in the Sikh Empire's rise to power. His ability to forge partnerships with regional tribes and leaders helped to strengthen Sikh authority over the area. These agreements improved the Sikh Empire's military capabilities and insured the local populaces' cooperation, making it simpler to rule the conquered lands.

The Afghan armies' loss in the Battle of Jamrud in 1837 was one of Nalwa's most important military victories. The strong Dost Mohammad Khan was in command of the Afghan army, which aimed to retake Peshawar from Sikh rule. However, the Afghan approach was halted by Nalwa's astute strategic judgment and staunch defense of the Jamrud Fort. Nalwa successfully held the fort despite having a significant numerical disadvantage, suffering significant losses among the Afghan men. Jamrud's Afghan loss signaled a sea change in the balance of power in the area and cemented Sikh control in the Northwest Frontier Province.

The Sikh Empire's frontiers were protected by Nalwa's military accomplishments and creative strategies, which also helped the empire to grow in scope and influence. He was a powerful military commander because of his capacity to adjust to shifting conditions, take advantage of his enemies' vulnerabilities, and make most of the resources at his disposal. Nalwa distinguished himself as one of the most respected people in the history of the Sikh Empire and left a lasting legacy in the annals of combat thanks to his tactical genius, strategic vision, and steadfast fortitude.

Chapter 4

The Battle of Jamrud

4.1 Context and significance of the Battle of Jamrud

A pivotal moment in the history of the Sikh Empire and the surrounding area was the Battle of Jamrud, which took place on April 30, 1837. The conflict pitted the Sikh troops under Sardar Hari Singh Nalwa against the Afghan army under Dost Mohammad Khan at the Jamrud Fort in modern-day Pakistan, close to the Khyber Pass.

Control of the key Khyber Pass, a vital economic and military route linking the Indian subcontinent with Central Asia, was at stake in the conflict. Under Maharaja Ranjit Singh's direction, the Sikh Empire had already taken possession of the Khyber Pass, allowing them to continue to rule the Northwest Frontier Province and defend their lands from prospective assaults.

But after Maharaja Ranjit Singh's passing in 1839, the Sikh Empire experienced internal power conflicts and a loss of leadership. Dost Mohammad Khan, the Afghan emir, saw a chance to retake the territory and launched an attack against the Sikhs in an effort to retake Peshawar and the surrounding districts.

The conclusion of this Afghan effort to drive the Sikhs from the Khyber Pass was the Battle of Jamrud. Around 12,000 Afghan warriors fought a mighty Sikh army of around 6,000 soldiers under the command of Sardar Hari Singh Nalwa, who was renowned for his tactical acumen and defensive strength.

The result of the battle of Jamrud and its effects on the regional power dynamics are what make it significant. Nalwa's strategic brilliance and staunch defense of the Jamrud Fort, while being vastly outnumbered, caused several losses among the Afghan men and stopped their assault. The conflict included heavy fighting and hand-to-hand warfare that continued for many hours.

In the end, the Afghan forces were able to penetrate the fort's outer walls, but Nalwa's soldiers put up a valiant fight and severely damaged their adversaries. Nalwa was critically wounded at a crucial second, but his troops kept fighting and repelled the Afghan army.

The Sikh Empire successfully defended the Jamrud Fort and maintained control of the Khyber Pass despite the fact that the conflict came to a standstill. This victory served as proof of Nalwa's tactical skill and the Sikh army's combat prowess.

The consequences of the Battle of Jamrud were felt across the area. As a result, Sikh supremacy in the Northwest Frontier Province was cemented, and additional Afghan invasions into Sikh territory were discouraged. Controlling the Khyber Pass allowed the Sikh Empire to keep access to important commercial routes and increased their geopolitical might.

The war also made the Khyber Pass more significant as a military junction and a doorway to Central Asia. The Sikh Empire was able to project its dominance and preserve regional security because to its control over this vital gateway.

But the Sikh Empire's demise was also heralded by the Battle of Jamrud. The loss of Nalwa, a respected military commander, inflicted a heavy blow to the Sikh soldiers and weakened their ability to defend the area. The Sikh Empire finally fell apart due to internal strife and outside influences, and Punjab was subsequently annexed by the British in 1849.

An important turning point in the history of the Sikh Empire and the conflict for control of the Khyber Pass was the Battle of Jamrud. It demonstrated both the tenacity of the Sikh army and the tactical genius of Sardar Hari Singh Nalwa. Even though it ended in a draw, the conflict had wider ramifications for the balance of power in the area, establishing Sikh supremacy in the Northwest Frontier Province and stressing the importance of the Khyber Pass from a strategic standpoint.

4.2 Nalwa's preparations and defensive strategies

Sardar Hari Singh Nalwa was renowned for his thorough planning and defensive tactics, which were essential to his effective defense of fortifications and territory. His meticulous preparation and execution of defensive measures demonstrated his military savvy and capacity to foresee and successfully repel enemy assaults.

Building and fortifying important defense sites was one of the main components of Nalwa's preparations. He understood the value of fortified fortifications in securing critical routes and defending lands. Numerous forts were built by Nalwa, notably the renowned Jamrud Fort, which functioned as a strong defensive stronghold. These forts were positioned carefully to provide a distinct advantage in terms of geography and to build solid defensive lines that slowed down enemy assaults.

Nalwa gave careful consideration to securing these buildings. He made certain that they had strong defensive elements including high walls, watchtowers, gun emplacements, and well-guarded gateways. The capacity to endure protracted sieges and fend off enemy attacks were tactical concerns included into the building of these forts. Nalwa's concentration on defense enabled his men to repel enemy assaults while being much outnumbered.

Nalwa strengthened the security of his territory by using a variety of defensive tactics in addition to fortifications. He built a network of watchtowers and outposts to improve observation and alerting capabilities. His soldiers were able to quickly identify enemy movements because to these well placed observation stations. These defensive tactics were enhanced by the efficient employment of scouts and intelligence networks, which delivered vital information about enemy troop movements and intentions.

Nalwa also understood the value of logistics and supply chains in maintaining defensive operations. In order to assure a consistent flow of necessary supplies, such as food, ammunition, and reinforcements, he made steps to secure and maintain supply channels. His men were able to successfully hold their defensive positions over lengthy sieges because to these logistical preparations.

Nalwa set up a system of tactical soldier placement and deployment to improve the defense of his domains. He strategically deployed his men, placing them in vital defense positions and giving them clear job descriptions. This made it possible for a coordinated defense, in which several troops supported one another and cleverly made use of the terrain. Nalwa's tactical deployment made sure that his soldiers were ready to undertake successful defensive operations and repel any prospective enemy offensives.

To increase the efficiency of his soldiers, Nalwa also used creative defense strategies. He made use of the area's rough topography to impede enemy advances by erecting natural barriers. Nalwa successfully interrupted enemy supply lines, caused fatalities, and demoralized his opponents by taking advantage of defensive locations and using guerilla warfare techniques.

In addition to showcasing his military might, Nalwa's preparations and defensive plans also built a strong barrier against outside threats. His ability to efficiently secure and retain control over his domains was made possible by his attention to fortifications, surveillance, logistics, soldier deployment, and cutting-edge tactics. These preparations helped the Sikh Empire endure besiegements, stave off enemy attacks, and win significant triumphs.

Sardar Singh Hari Nalwa's detailed planning and defense tactics demonstrated his superior military skills. His focus on fortifications, surveillance, logistics, strategic deployment, and cutting-edge tactics showed his capacity to foresee and successfully repel enemy assaults. Nalwa's defensive strategies demonstrated his military prowess and protected the interests of the Sikh Empire. They were essential to the effective defense of fortifications and territory.

4.3 The decisive victory over the Afghan forces

Nalwa strategically positioned his men despite being outnumbered and came up with a defensive plan that capitalized on the advantages of both his soldiers and the fortified location of the Jamrud Fort. He built a strong defense against the Afghan assault by using the fort's defensive strengths and the surrounding terrain.

The Afghan soldiers made many efforts to breach the fort's fortifications, and the combat was hard and violent. But Nalwa's soldiers maintained their position, displaying astounding courage, focus, and fortitude. The Sikhs dealt a crushing defeat to the Afghans by repelling wave after wave of attacks.

Nalwa himself was fatally wounded at a vital phase of the war while commanding his soldiers from the front lines. But despite his wound, his men persisted in their bravery in the face of it, motivated by his leadership. They came together under the leadership of their seasoned commanders and stood their ground against the Afghan soldiers.

Even with their greater numerical advantage, the Afghan soldiers were unable to successfully penetrate the fort's fortifications after many hours of intense fighting. They ultimately withdrew after suffering significant casualties and the Sikh army's tenacious fight, failing to complete their mission of retaking the fort and the surrounding areas.

The triumph at Jamrud was a tribute to Nalwa's tactical acumen, the courage of his soldiers, and the efficacy of their defensive preparations. The Sikh warriors headed by Nalwa successfully stopped the Afghan attack and guarded their citadel despite being outnumbered and facing a tough foe.

This victory's importance cannot be emphasized. In addition to preserving the Sikh Empire's grip over the Northwest Frontier Province and the strategically significant Khyber Pass, it also made a strong statement about the Sikh people's fortitude and might to the Afghan army and other nearby nations.

Sardar Hari Singh Nalwa's military skill and strategic insight were on display at the Battle of Jamrud. His tactical acumen and leadership abilities were on full display as he inspired his soldiers, came up with a successful defense plan, and managed to fend off a stronger army. The victory further strengthened the Sikh soldiers' position in the area and discouraged any Afghan assaults by boosting their morale and confidence.

Sardar Hari Singh Nalwa's stunning victory against the Afghan soldiers at the Battle of Jamrud was evidence of both his tactical prowess and the combat prowess of the Sikh army. With this triumph, the Sikh warriors proved their tenacity and bravery while securing their authority over the Khyber Pass and the Northwest Frontier Province. The fort was successfully defended under Nalwa's command, and thus helped to shape the regional power structure and establish the Sikh Empire's dominance.

Chapter 5

Nalwa's Administrative Contributions

5.1 Role as the governor of Peshawar

In the Sikh Empire, Sardar Hari Singh Nalwa was given the important administrative and strategic role of governor of Peshawar. His selection as governor demonstrated Maharaja Ranjit Singh, the head of the Sikh Empire, confidence in Nalwa's skills as a military commander and administrator.

Nalwa was charged with overseeing the administration of the area, preserving peace, and defending the interests of the Sikh Empire as governor of Peshawar. He took over a region that had a complicated history of political rivalry and internal disputes in addition to being varied in terms of its ethnic and cultural makeup.

To create and maintain peace and order in the area was one of Nalwa's principal goals as governor. He put in place a strict and just government, making sure that justice was served and disagreements were arbitrated properly. Respect among the local populace and aid in maintaining peace in the area came from his reputation as a strict but fair ruler.

Nalwa also gave attention to Peshawar's economic growth. He started a number of infrastructure initiatives, such as the building of roads, bridges, and irrigation canals, which aided in commerce and enhanced communication in the area. His efforts increased agriculture and trade, which increased the wealth of the territory he governed.

Nalwa was also acutely aware of the need of preserving good relations with the nearby tribes and villages. He honored the various people under his control's cultures, traditions, and religious convictions. Nalwa pursued alliances and collaboration with significant tribal leaders by pursuing a diplomatic and engagement strategy. This strategy not only promoted stability but also improved administration and defense-related collaboration.

Nalwa continued to give the region's defense first priority while serving as governor. In order to keep Peshawar safe from outside attacks, he strengthened and extensively fortified important locations and forts. The province was more stable and secure during Nalwa's rule because of his knowledge of defense tactics and dedication to defending the interests of the Sikh Empire.

Nalwa's term as governor of Peshawar was distinguished by his efficient administration, tenacious leadership, and dedication to the well-being of the populace. His efforts to upgrade the region's infrastructure, encourage economic development, and uphold law and order brought stability and prosperity to the area. His reasonable and fair reign, together with his military experience, won him the respect and adoration of the local populace.

Nalwa's term as governor, however, was sadly cut short. Nalwa died from his combat wounds in 1837, not long after the combat of Jamrud. He had established himself as a skilled and well-respected leader, therefore his death was a big loss for the Sikh Empire and the area.

Sardar Singh Hari Nalwa's tenure as the governor of Peshawar was distinguished by his skillful administration, emphasis on development, and dedication to security. During his reign, the area saw stability, economic expansion, and better governance. Nalwa's just and equitable administration, together with his military prowess, helped to secure Peshawar's prosperity and safety under the Sikh Empire.

5.2 Introduction of reforms and infrastructure development

Sardar Hari Singh Nalwa oversaw a number of changes as the governor of Peshawar and led major infrastructure development initiatives. Nalwa initiated these steps to strengthen governance, foster economic development, and improve the standard of living for those living under his authority after seeing the need to modernize and improve the area.

The implementation of administrative changes was one of Nalwa's primary areas of attention. His goals were to make the governance system more efficient, assure equitable and fair administration, and simplify it. Nalwa put rules in place to thwart corruption, promote openness, and provide a framework for official responsibility. These changes enabled effective governance and the prompt provision of public services in addition to fostering trust in the administration.

Nalwa also gave high priority to infrastructure development since he understood how important it was for promoting connectivity and fostering economic progress. He started building roads, bridges, and canals to improve the area's transportation and communication. These infrastructural improvements aided commerce, increased agricultural output, and promoted trade. Nalwa also concentrated on improving irrigation systems to support agriculture, which was the main source of income for the community.

Additionally, Nalwa worked to update Peshawar's military and defensive infrastructure. He improved the region's defense capabilities by fortifying already-existing forts and building new defensive buildings. These steps were taken to protect the region from outside dangers and to uphold the security of the Sikh Empire's interests. Peshawar was kept well-defended and fortified because to Nalwa's focus on defensive infrastructure.

Nalwa was dedicated to advancing cultural and educational advancement in addition to administrative and physical changes. He supported the creation of educational institutions like schools that would provide the local populace the chance to learn new things. In order to empower the populace and prepare them for a brighter future, Nalwa supported education. Additionally, he supported literature, the arts, and other cultural pursuits, fostering Peshawar's thriving cultural scene.

Peshawar and the surrounding area saw a radical transformation as a result of Nalwa's reforms and infrastructure development projects. His leadership and vision established the groundwork for development and prosperity. Administrative changes were implemented, which simplified administration, increased effectiveness, and strengthened the provision of public services. Projects to build the infrastructure encouraged commerce, enhanced connectivity, and accelerated economic growth. The region's security was assured by a concentration on defensive infrastructure, while educational and cultural activities promoted intellectual development and cultural enrichment.

Sardar Singh Hari Nalwa's implementation of reforms and the building of new infrastructure in Peshawar demonstrated his dedication to effective leadership, burgeoning economies, and the welfare of the populace. His bold thinking and decisive actions had a long-lasting effect on the area and helped pave the way for its further expansion and success. The infrastructural improvements and reforms implemented by Nalwa not only improved the standard of living for the populace but also helped progress the Sikh Empire as a whole.

5.3 Promotion of trade and commerce in the region

Under his leadership, Sardar Hari Singh Nalwa understood the need of fostering trade and business in the area. Nalwa put in place measures to enable and promote commercial operations after realizing the importance of a healthy economy for the well-being of the populace and the general development of the region.

The development of the transportation infrastructure was one of the important actions made by Nalwa. He made investments in the building and upkeep of the roads, bridges, and canals that linked the various parts of the realm and aided in the transportation of products. These infrastructural improvements enhanced accessibility, decreased transportation costs, and encouraged commerce between Peshawar and other regions.

Nalwa also made an effort to make trade routes more secure. He understood the importance of merchant and product safety to the expansion of trade. He reinforced major tunnels, stationed soldiers beside trade routes, and set up checkpoints to deter theft and provide merchants security in order to guarantee safe trading routes. These safety precautions gave traders more confidence and propelled them into international trading.

Additionally, Nalwa aggressively encouraged the development of marketplaces and trade hubs. He promoted the expansion of neighborhood markets, drawing traders from various areas and easing the trade of products and services. Nalwa also promoted cross-border commerce and commercial links with neighboring nations. To encourage a business-friendly atmosphere, he negotiated beneficial trade agreements and removed pointless obstacles like high taxes and tariffs.

Nalwa was aware of how crucial a stable currency was for commerce. He put in place procedures to control and harmonize the monetary system, making sure that businesspeople could interact with confidence and without worrying about fake money. The currency's stability made trading more easier and fueled economic expansion.

Additionally, Nalwa promoted the development of local industry and crafts. He encouraged the development of high-quality items that could be sold locally and exported to other areas by offering incentives and assistance to artists and craftspeople. In addition to boosting economic activity, this support for local businesses also helped the area thrive as a whole.

Nalwa was instrumental in enhancing the economic prosperity of Peshawar and the neighboring regions by fostering trade and commerce. Increased job possibilities, higher living standards, and the interchange of commodities and ideas were all benefits of growing commerce. Additionally, it promoted cross-cultural interaction and aided in the region's general growth.

Sardar Singh Hari The region's economic development and increased standard of living were both aided by Nalwa's encouragement of trade and commerce. Nalwa established an atmosphere that was favorable to trade and business via the development of infrastructure, improved security measures, support for markets, and the expansion of businesses. His initiatives made the area more prosperous and guaranteed Peshawar's status as a bustling commercial hub within the Sikh Empire.

Chapter 6

The Relationship between the Sikh Empire and Afghanistan

6.1 Historical interactions and conflicts

Afghanistan has always been a meeting place for many cultures, and it has had many exchanges and wars with surrounding nations and forces. The dynamics of the nation's political, social, and cultural systems have been affected by these exchanges throughout its history.

One of Afghanistan's first historical encounters may be found in prehistoric periods, when the country was strategically located along trade routes between Central Asia, the Indian subcontinent, and the Middle East. As a consequence, Afghanistan developed into a crossroads of civilizations, drawing traders, businesspeople, and tourists from all over the globe. The emergence of a multicultural civilization with influences from Persia, India, Central Asia, and other places was facilitated by this cross-cultural interaction.

Afghanistan was a sought-after region for several empires and powers due to its strategic position and abundant resources. The area has seen invasions and wars from empires including the Islamic Caliphates, the Mauryan Empire of India, the Persian Achaemenids, and the Greek

Seleucids throughout history. These invasions often led to local communities' resistance as well as cultural and political assimilation.

Afghanistan served as a hub for the spread of Islam throughout the Middle Ages and saw the establishment and fall of several Islamic kingdoms. The Ghaznavids, Ghorids, and Timurids were only a few of the Islamic kingdoms that were founded in the area. In addition to introducing Islam to the area, these dynasties promoted the growth of literature, art, and architecture.

In more recent times, throughout the 19th and 20th centuries, Afghanistan had major wars and relations with foreign countries. The nation turned into a theater of conflict for the Great Game, a geopolitical conflict between the Russian and British empires. The Russians wanted to increase their influence in Central Asia, while the British wanted to defend their Indian Empire by keeping control over Afghanistan. Due to this competition, Afghanistan sometimes saw military incursions, political intrigue, and diplomatic manipulation.

The 20th century saw substantial unrest in Afghanistan as well, notably during the Cold War era. The nation was used as a battlefield for proxies between the US and the USSR. A communist takeover in Afghanistan in the late 1970s prompted Soviet involvement, which resulted in a 10-year war known as the Soviet-Afghan War. During this struggle, many nations, including the United States, provided assistance to the Afghan resistance, also known as the mujahideen. After the Soviet Union withdrew in

1989, Afghanistan had a protracted era of instability and civil war as a result of domestic conflict.

After the September 11 attacks in 2001, Afghanistan once again became the focus of global interest in the early 21st century. In order to destroy terrorist networks and overthrow the Taliban government in Afghanistan, a coalition headed by the United States began a military operation. There were substantial military operations, political changes, and attempts at stability and rebuilding as a consequence of the subsequent struggle, known as the War in Afghanistan.

Afghanistan has seen several contacts and wars with nearby nations and powerful nations throughout its history. The cultural environment of the nation, the political climate, and the quality of life for its citizens have all been changed by these encounters. Afghanistan is a zone of intrigue and conflict in the contemporary world because to its strategic position, rich history, and geopolitical relevance.

6.2 Nalwa's diplomacy and negotiations with Afghan leaders

While serving as the governor of Peshawar, Sardar Hari Singh Nalwa, who was renowned for his military strength, also shown his ability to negotiate with Afghan authorities. Nalwa used diplomacy to protect the interests of the Sikh Empire and promote collaboration with Afghan authorities because he recognized the need of keeping stable relations with neighboring countries.

Engagement with Afghan tribal chiefs was one of Nalwa's diplomatic achievements. Nalwa tried to form alliances with other tribes and build relationships based on respect and understanding since he was aware of the influence and authority these tribal leaders had in the area. He went on diplomatic missions, meeting with powerful Afghan figures to broker accords, create communication lines, and negotiate peace.

Nalwa was aware of the importance of local religious and cultural sensibilities. He showed cultural sensitivity and respect for the Afghan people's traditions and customs by making an attempt to comprehend their way of life. Through the development of trust and a positive relationship with Afghan officials, this strategy served to foster a cooperative atmosphere for diplomacy and talks.

Nalwa also used his military victories as leverage in talks. His successes against Afghan troops and his image as a fierce fighter helped him gain credibility and strengthen his position in negotiations with foreign governments. Afghan officials were more willing to negotiate and find peaceful solutions than to risk escalating the conflict since they were aware of Nalwa's military might.

Nalwa's diplomatic activities included settling conflicts and disagreements within the area. In tribal disputes, he served as a mediator, organizing talks and attempting to find amicable solutions. He was respected by several sides for his impartiality and dedication to justice, which enabled him to play a significant part in settling conflicts and preserving peace.

Nalwa also recognized the value of business links in advancing diplomatic relations. He saw that trade and business might be used to improve connections between the Sikh Empire and Afghanistan. Nalwa promoted international commerce, established trade agreements, and made it easier for traders and products to travel. These business dealings acted as a springboard for diplomatic ties and promoted mutual confidence and collaboration.

Sardar Singh Hari Nalwa's diplomacy and talks with the Afghan government's officials were distinguished by a blend of military might, cultural sensitivity, and economic concerns. His diplomatic initiatives attempted to enhance collaboration between the Sikh Empire and Afghanistan, develop peaceful ties, and settle disputes. Through his diplomatic efforts, Nalwa showed that he was capable of navigating tricky political situations, protecting the interests of the Sikh Empire, and preserving regional peace.

6.3 Changing dynamics and tensions between the two powers

Sardar Hari Singh Nalwa's reign was marked by shifting dynamics and tensions in the Sikh Empire's ties with Afghanistan. Despite Nalwa's diplomatic abilities and his involvement in talks with Afghan authorities, there were underlying issues and long-standing animosities between the two countries that periodically hampered relations.

The historical rivalry between the Afghan and Sikh people was one of the important elements causing tensions between the Sikh Empire and Afghanistan. The Sikhs, commanded by Maharaja Ranjit Singh, wanted to increase their power and territory in the area, which often put them in opposition to the Afghan kings. Building confidence and forming long-lasting coalitions was difficult because of this rivalry's historical animosities and territorial disputes.

The relationship was further complicated by Afghanistan's geopolitical position and its desire for independence. Afghanistan fought to preserve its independence and resisted outside interference as a buffer state between rival powers. Conflicts and tensions sometimes resulted from this quest for autonomy running afoul of the Sikh Empire's expansionist goals.

The evolving relationships between the Sikh Empire and Afghanistan were also influenced by religion. With its origins in the Punjab area and the Sikh religion, the Sikh Empire had a distinctive religious identity that was different from Afghanistan's mostly Muslim populace. Because religious conflicts might affect political and social relations, there was periodically concern and distrust between the two powers as a result of this theological difference.

The strategic significance of Peshawar and the areas around it further increased the complexity of the connection. Peshawar was a sought-after region for both the Sikh Empire and Afghanistan due to its strategic location at the intersection of important trade routes. Conflicts and power struggles developed as a consequence of disagreements about control and influence over this area.

Despite these conflicts, there were other times when the Sikh Empire and Afghanistan were friendly and coexisted peacefully. Leaders like Sardar Hari Singh Nalwa led diplomatic missions and discussions with the objective of establishing commercial deals, resolving disputes, and finding common ground. Nalwa's diplomatic efforts were crucial in promoting understanding and, at least temporarily, easing tensions between the two countries.

The shifting relationships between the Sikh Empire and Afghanistan remained weak and complicated, nevertheless. The relationship was nevertheless impacted by underlying historical rivalries, territory conflicts, and divergent ambitions for independence and influence. These elements made it difficult for the relationship to remain stable over the long run since they led to a feeling of uncertainty and sporadic escalation of stress.

Under Sardar Hari Singh Nalwa, the dynamics and tensions in the relationship between the Sikh Empire and Afghanistan changed often. The relations between the two empires were impacted by historical rivalries, territory conflicts, religious disagreements, and geopolitical goals. Although discussions and diplomatic attempts were made to promote collaboration, the relationship was often stressed by the underlying difficulties and historical considerations. The shifting dynamics and tensions between the Sikh Empire and Afghanistan during that time period were a reflection of the region's overall geopolitical environment.

Chapter 7

Nalwa's Military Campaigns in Afghanistan

7.1 Expansion of the Sikh Empire into Afghan territories

During the rule of Maharaja Ranjit Singh, the Sikh Empire expanded into Afghan territory, which was a momentous development and had a considerable impact on the geopolitical environment of the area. Under the direction of Maharaja Ranjit Singh and his dependable generals, such Sardar Hari Singh Nalwa, the Sikh Empire aimed to bolster its position and extend its influence outside of the Punjab.

Securing its western boundary and defending its realms from outside threats was one of the Sikh Empire's top priorities. Due to their geographic position and closeness to the center of the Sikh Empire, the Afghan regions, notably the Peshawar area, possessed strategic significance. The Sikh Empire sought to construct a buffer zone, build a solid defensive posture, and take control of important trade routes by pushing into Afghan territory.

There were obstacles encountered with the advance into Afghani territory. Afghan kings, tribal chiefs, and residents vigorously fought Sikh incursions into their domains. They saw the Sikh Empire as an outside force attempting to exercise influence and authority over their country. The

Sikh army and the Afghan resistance engaged in multiple battles as a result of this resistance.

The Sikh Empire's progress into Afghan territory was greatly aided by Sardar Hari Singh Nalwa. He oversaw numerous successful military operations while serving as the governor of Peshawar, seizing vital forts and putting the Sikhs in charge of significant regions. The Sikh Empire was able to overcome Afghan opposition because to Nalwa's military strength, creative strategies, and excellent leadership.

The administration and governance of these areas saw considerable changes as a result of the Sikh Empire's advance into Afghan territory. The newly acquired regions were governed by Sikh administrators, who also made an attempt to incorporate them into the larger Sikh administrative framework. To retain dominance and guarantee the efficient operation of the acquired areas, Sikh institutions, such as the Sikh army and administrative systems, were built.

Aside from political effects, the Sikh Empire's expansion into Afghanistan had social and cultural repercussions. Sikh and Hindu immigrants from the Punjab area were encouraged by the Sikh authorities to go to the newly conquered lands. The establishment of the Punjabi Sikh and Hindu communities in the Afghan regions resulted in demographic shifts and cultural interchange. However, it also led to difficulties and cultural misunderstandings with the area's mostly Muslim populace.

Even though the Sikh Empire was able to seize control of substantial swaths of Afghan territory, the grip on these areas was shaky. The Sikh government faced continual difficulties because to the rough terrain, tribal dynamics, and persistent hostility from Afghan organizations. The Afghan lands that the Sikh Empire conquered retained some autonomy and their own unique cultural identities, and they were not entirely incorporated into the core Sikh domains.

The history of the area was significantly impacted by the Sikh Empire's advance into Afghani territory. It impacted the ensuing power battles in the area and changed the political dynamics as well as the cultural environment. For a while, the Sikh Empire's presence in Afghanistan acted as a counterweight to other regional powers and aided in maintaining geopolitical peace in the region.

A crucial turning point in the history of the area was the expansion of the Sikh Empire into Afghan territory under Maharaja Ranjit Singh, under the direction of people like Sardar Hari Singh Nalwa. By expanding into Afghan territory, the Sikh Empire aimed to establish dominance, defend its western boundary, and safeguard its interests. The Sikh Empire overcame obstacles and opposition to establish authority over significant territories, resulting in changes to management, administration, and demography. The geopolitical environment of the area was formed by the expansion into Afghan territory, which also had a long-lasting effect on the history of Afghanistan and the Sikh Empire.

7.2 Challenges faced and victories achieved

Under Sardar Hari Singh Nalwa's direction, the Sikh Empire's advance into Afghanistan wasn't without its difficulties. To win their triumphs, the Sikh armies had to overcome a number of challenges and impediments.

The intense opposition from Afghan tribal elders and the local community was one of the main difficulties. The Afghans, who were renowned for their combat skills and familiarity with the difficult terrain, presented a serious threat to the Sikh troops. They vigorously resisted Sikh incursion since they were firmly established in their homeland. The Sikh soldiers struggled to establish a stable footing in the area as a result of this resistance, which resulted in protracted conflicts and guerrilla warfare.

The difficult terrain of Afghanistan presented the Sikh army with additional difficulties. Military operations were difficult and exhausting due to the challenging terrain, which included steep valleys and rough mountains. To get where they needed to go, the Sikh soldiers had to negotiate perilous mountain routes, ford rivers, and travel through difficult terrain. Because of this topographical diversity, military battles took longer to complete and the Sikh soldiers were more vulnerable to ambushes and guerilla assaults.

Additionally, there were logistical difficulties throughout the invasions of Afghani territory. The Sikh troops found it difficult to maintain their operations because of the great distances, a lack of infrastructure, and constrained supply lines. They had to depend on effective communication networks, build supply chains, and adjust to the challenging local conditions. It took careful preparation, ingenuity, and adaptation to get beyond these logistical obstacles.

The Sikh army, led by Sardar Hari Singh Nalwa, overcame these obstacles to win a number of important battles in Afghanistan. The success of these operations was greatly influenced by Nalwa's military genius, strategic insight, and creative tactics.

The 1837 seizure of Jamrud, a key strategic fortification, was one of the major successes. A key bastion protecting the entrance to the Khyber Pass, an important commercial and transit route, was the citadel. Nalwa oversaw a well-organized assault that included an artillery barrage, infantry assaults, and strategic movements. The Sikh soldiers were able to get through the fortifications, winning a major battle that not only increased the Sikh Empire's dominance but also significantly weakened the Afghan resistance.

Another outstanding accomplishment was the seizure of Peshawar's stronghold in 1834. Peshawar was a key strategic and commercial location since it was a gateway to Central Asia and Afghanistan. To take possession of the citadel, the Sikh army staged a number of military battles and sieges under Nalwa's direction. The Sikh armies prevailed after a protracted period of fighting and resistance, securing full control over Peshawar and establishing Sikh rule in the area.

The successes won by the Sikh armies under Nalwa's command not only increased the Sikh Empire's realms of influence, but also showed their military fortitude and tenacity. These conquests resulted in important geopolitical shifts that made the Sikh Empire the dominating force in the area and reduced the dominance of Afghan kings and tribes.

The Sikh troops' achievements in Afghanistan also had larger ramifications for regional stability. A brief era of relative peace and security in the area was facilitated by the Sikh Empire's presence in Afghani territory, which acted as a counterweight to other regional forces.

There were difficulties throughout the Sikh soldiers' battles in Afghanistan under the command of Sardar Hari Singh Nalwa. Significant barriers were the opposition of Afghan tribes, challenging terrain, and logistical difficulties. But because to Nalwa's military prowess and strategic insight, the Sikh armies won impressive successes, taking control of important fortifications, and extending their influence. These triumphs changed the regional power balances and ushered in a time of stability. The operations in Afghanistan that Nalwa oversaw provide as evidence of the Sikh Empire's strength and tenacity on the battlefield.

7.3 Nalwa's influence on the geopolitical landscape

Sardar Singh Hari The geopolitical environment of the area was significantly and widely impacted by Nalwa. Nalwa was a significant military leader and the governor of Peshawar during his time, and he had a significant impact on the geopolitical landscape.

First off, the Sikh Empire in the area gained strength and influence as a result of Nalwa's military victories and territory expansion. His inventive strategies and strategic vision allowed him to take control of important areas, including Peshawar and other regions of Pakistan's Khyber Pakhtunkhwa province at the time. The Sikh Empire's borders were expanded through these victories, which also gave the Sikhs major authority over areas of Afghanistan.

Nalwa's impact on world politics extended beyond its territorial victories. He participated in conversations with Afghan tribal chiefs and local populations because he recognized the value of diplomatic connections. His diplomatic prowess and capacity for forging alliances contributed to regional peace and eased tensions between the Sikh Empire and Afghanistan. Nalwa sought to promote goodwill and a stable geopolitical climate via his diplomatic activities.

Additionally, Nalwa's administrative and governmental changes in the areas under his rule had a long-lasting effect on the geopolitical environment. He enacted policies to foster business and trade, build infrastructure, and enhance government structures. The Sikh Empire's power was bolstered and its place in the greater geopolitical environment was improved by these activities, which also helped the region's economy flourish and thrive.

The fact that Nalwa was the governor of Peshawar contributed to the area's feeling of security and stability. His capable military leadership served as a deterrence to outside attack and guaranteed the safeguarding of the Sikh Empire's interests. The geopolitical environment changed as a result of this stability and security, which attracted traders, merchants, and tourists to the area and promoted commerce and cultural interactions.

Furthermore, Nalwa's impact went beyond the local geopolitical context of the Afghan and Sikh Empires. His conquests and reputation as a fierce fighter spread across the area, earning him fame and changing how other nations saw the Sikh Empire. Under Nalwa's direction, the

Sikh Empire rose to prominence as a regional power, exercising its influence and having an effect on the balance of power in a wider geopolitical context.

Nalwa made contributions to geopolitics that extended beyond his tenure as governor of Peshawar. His military triumphs and diplomatic initiatives created the groundwork for later regional events. The lands Nalwa acquired were an essential aspect of the Sikh Empire, helping to define its borders and sphere of influence for decades to come.

Sardar Singh Hari Nalwa had a significant impact on the geopolitical environment. His military victories, diplomatic initiatives, and administrative improvements completely altered the regional power balance. The Sikh Empire's accomplishments under Nalwa expanded its realm, consolidated its power, and created an atmosphere of peace and security. His influence reverberated across the area, affecting the geopolitical landscape and the balance of power.

Chapter 8

The Siege of Multan

8.1 Background of the conflict and reasons for the siege

An important occasion that occurred in 1837, during the height of the Sikh Empire's push into Afghanistan, was the Siege of Jamrud. The geopolitical setting and the underlying causes of the hostilities between the Sikh Empire and the Afghan tribes must be taken into account in order to comprehend the history of the war and the justifications for the siege.

The Sikh Empire's intention to take control of the Khyber Pass was one of the main causes of the battle. The Khyber Pass is a significant mountain pass that connects the Indian subcontinent with Afghanistan and Central Asia. It is situated in the contemporary Pakistani state of Khyber Pakhtunkhwa. The Sikh Empire understood the strategic importance of this route since it regulated commerce and served as a point of entry for military operations into Afghanistan.

The Afghan tribes who lived in the area surrounding Jamrud, especially the Afridis, strongly fought Sikh incursions into their domains. They saw the existence of the Sikh Empire as a danger to their independence and way of life. The Afridis, who were renowned for their independence and military traditions, were adamant about defending their territory and restraining Sikh rule. This conflict of goals and objectives produced an unstable scenario that finally resulted in the siege.

The historical rivalries and wars between Afghans and Sikhs have contributed to the animosity between the two groups. Territorial conflicts and power struggles between Afghans and Sikhs date back to the reign of Ahmad Shah Durrani, the country's founding father. The Afghan tribes saw the Sikh Empire's progress into their country as a continuation of their long-standing rivalry, which fueled their hostility and resistance.

Furthermore, the tense ties between the Sikhs and Afghans were a result of religious and cultural differences. The majority of people in the Sikh Empire were Sikh and Hindu, but the Afghan tribes followed Sunni Islam. There was mistrust and hostility between the two groups as a result of these religious and cultural differences.

The Sikh Empire's military aspirations and the Afghan tribes' steadfast commitment to protect their territory may be held responsible for the particular causes of the siege of Jamrud. Sardar Hari Singh Nalwa led the Sikh troops as they made an effort to seize the Khyber Pass and establish a secure presence in the area. The Afridis, under the leadership of their tribal chiefs, opposed Sikh incursions and resisted submitting to Sikh control.

These conflicts and competing interests culminated in the siege of Jamrud. The Sikh soldiers began an attempt to take control of Jamrud, a strategically important citadel that defended the Khyber Pass's entrance. The Afridis had a superior defensive posture because to the stronghold' high location. Despite having a larger troop and better weaponry, the Afridis put up a fierce and tenacious fight against the Sikh soldiers.

Multiple weeks of heavy combat and artillery fire exchanged throughout the siege. Throughout the fight, courage and persistence were demonstrated by both sides. However, the Sikh soldiers were unable to take the castle because of the Afridis' tenacious resistance. There was no apparent winner in the siege, which came to a standstill.

The Sikh Empire's push into Afghan lands was complicated and difficult, as the siege of Jamrud demonstrated. It showed the Afghan tribes' tenacity and fortitude in protecting their country and their refusal to submit to Sikh rule. The siege highlighted the strategic significance of the Khyber Pass as well as the challenges the Sikh Empire had in gaining control of this important trading route.

The underlying tensions, old rivalries, and competing interests between the Sikh Empire and the Afghan tribes led to the siege of Jamrud. The Afghan tribes wanted to retain their independence and resisted foreign rule, but the Sikh Empire's plans to dominate the Khyber Pass conflicted with those goals. The siege brought to light the geopolitical landscape's complexity and the difficulties the Sikh Empire faced in extending its authority into Afghan territory.

8.2 Nalwa's strategies and tactics during the siege

Sardar Hari Singh Nalwa used a variety of plans and tactics to attempt to take the citadel and defeat the tenacious resistance of the Afridis during the Siege of Jamrud. Nalwa, who was renowned for his military prowess and creative thought, modified his strategy to fit the difficult conditions of the siege.

The creation of reinforced trenches and siege works was one of the main tactics Nalwa used. Nalwa gave the order to build trenches and earthworks to defend his own troops as they moved closer to the stronghold after seeing how strong the Afridis' defenses were within the fortress. The Sikh soldiers were protected by these fortifications from the Afridis' arrows, guns, and cannon fire. The Sikh soldiers could approach on the castle gradually and methodically from the trenches, reducing fatalities and increasing their prospects of victory.

Nalwa also used artillery to damage the Afridis' fortifications in addition to digging trenches. He carefully placed artillery and guns to attack the stronghold and break its defenses. In an effort to undermine the fortifications and create openings through which they might launch their attack, the Sikh troops launched a torrent of artillery fire. In order to weaken the Afridis' resistance and clear the way for the Sikh forces, artillery was used.

Nalwa also adopted a siege mentality tactic, isolating the stronghold and preventing the Afridis from receiving outside assistance. In order to keep the Afridis from obtaining reinforcements or supplies, he made sure that the Sikh soldiers had control of the surrounding districts.

Nalwa's goal in enforcing a blockade was to gradually undermine the defenders' morale, exhaust their supplies, and deepen their despair.

Nalwa also understood the value of psychological operations during the siege. He used a variety of psychological strategies to weaken the Afridis' determination and scare them. For instance, by displaying captured Afridi captives and performing martial arts exhibitions, the Sikh soldiers showed off their military might and proficiency. While concurrently raising the spirit of the Sikh forces, these demonstrations were meant to terrorize and demoralize the defenders.

Nalwa likewise took a deliberate and gradual strategy, knowing how impossible it would be to take the castle by frontal attack. He understood the Afridis' steadfast commitment to protecting their house and the formidability of their defensive stance. Nalwa chose to take a methodical, methodical strategy rather than launching a direct assault, concentrating on gradually weakening the defenses. With this strategy, he was able to save resources, reduce fatalities, and prepare for a successful attack when the time was right.

Nalwa had considerable difficulties throughout the siege despite his tactical mastery and strategic intelligence. The Afridis had an edge because to their strong fortifications, challenging terrain, and familiarity with the local topography. Because of the fortress's high location, the Sikh soldiers found it difficult to get an upper hand. Nalwa's patience and tenacity were also put to the test by the Afridis' guerrilla warfare tactics, which included ambushes and hit-and-run operations.

In the end, neither side emerged victorious from the siege of Jamrud with a clear advantage. Despite the Sikh army' best attempts, the Afridis managed to hold their position and successfully defend the citadel. The siege revealed the Afridis' tenacity and will as well as the difficulties Nalwa had in taking control of such a well-defended location.

During the Siege of Jamrud, Sardar Hari Singh Nalwa used a variety of techniques and tactics. These included digging defensive trenches, using artillery bombardment, adopting a siege mindset, engaging in psychological warfare, and taking a deliberate and methodical approach. The difficulties presented by the Afridis' fortifications and guerilla tactics eventually stopped the Sikh troops from taking the citadel, despite the fact that his ideas showed his tactical knowledge and creative thinking.

8.3 Outcome and impact on the Sikh-Afghan relations

The result of the Siege of Jamrud had a profound effect on Sikh-Afghan relations as well as the region's overall geopolitical environment. Although the siege came to a standstill, the events that followed had a significant impact.

First of all, the inability to conquer Jamrud and defeat the Afridis demonstrated the tenacity and steadfastness of the Afghan tribes in protecting their lands. It proved their steadfast will to fend against foreign hegemony and retain their independence. This strengthened the Afghan tribes' commitment to protect their territory and made subsequent Sikh efforts to colonize Afghan territory more difficult.

The conclusion of the siege also had an impact on the Sikh Empire's plans for territorial expansion and military conquest. The Sikh Empire's intentions to take control of the Khyber Pass and expand its influence into Afghanistan were foiled when they were unable to take the well defended citadel of Jamrud. The deadlock illustrated the challenges and complications of gaining military victory against resolute opposition and tough terrain.

The Siege of Jamrud also had a lasting impression on Sikh-Afghan ties. It increased hostilities and heightened tensions between the two sides. The breakdown of the siege and the ensuing departure of Sikh soldiers from the area were seen as a defeat for the Sikhs and a success for the Afghan resistance. The Afridis, encouraged by their effective defense, resisted Sikh incursions and were more eager to defend their lands.

The siege also led to a change in the regional geopolitical environment and the balance of power. It revealed the limitations of Sikh military might and sent a strong and resilient message to other regional powers, such as the British East India Company, about the Afghan tribes. This affected the plans and actions of nearby nations and had an impact on the future power dynamics in the area.

Additionally, the Siege of Jamrud and the ensuing hostilities between the Sikhs and the Afghans had an impact on the economy. Trade between the Indian subcontinent and Afghanistan was hampered by the closure of trade routes via the Khyber Pass. Both sides suffered as a result of this, since it reduced prospects for commerce and prosperity and hampered economic growth.

Long-term instability in the area was exacerbated by the Siege of Jamrud and tense Sikh-Afghan ties. Because of the Sikh Empire's decline and the continuous disputes between different Afghan tribes, conditions were favorable for outside meddling. This ultimately resulted in the Anglo-Sikh Wars and British annexation of the area.

The conclusion of the Siege of Jamrud had a profound effect on Sikh-Afghan relations as well as the regional geopolitical environment. The inability to take the castle of Jamrud revealed the tenacity and tenacity of the Afghan tribes, undermining Sikh aspirations and escalating hostilities. It had an impact on neighboring powers' strategy, changed the regional power dynamics, and affected the economy. The events of the siege paved the way for future wars and interventions while also contributing to the region's overall instability.

Chapter 9

Nalwa's Legacy in Punjab and Beyond

9.1 Impact on Sikh society and culture

Throughout the 19th century, the Siege of Jamrud and other Sikh-Afghan battles had a significant influence on Sikh society and culture. The incidents and their repercussions had an impact on a number of facets of Sikh life, such as identity, military customs, and ties between the Sikh community and the ruling class.

One of the most significant effects was the affirmation of Sikh pride and identity. Under Maharaja Ranjit Singh, the Sikh Empire aimed to increase and solidify Sikh dominance. Conflicts with the Afghan tribes, especially Jamrud's tenacious defense, acted as a spur for Sikh unification and a reaffirmation of their unique identity. The bravery of Sardar Hari Singh Nalwa and other Sikh soldiers served as an inspiration for the Sikh community, which became resilient and proud of itself.

The circumstances surrounding the Siege of Jamrud had an impact on Sikh military customs as well. Under Nalwa's command, the Sikh soldiers exhibited bravery, tactical innovation, and unflinching resolve. These characteristics were seen as essential to the Sikh martial culture and eventually gained respect within Sikh society. The Sikh troops' selfless acts throughout the battles solidified their image as fierce warriors.

Additionally, the Sikh-Afghan clashes and the Siege of Jamrud highlighted the difficulties the Sikh community experienced in maintaining their territorial integrity and defending their borders. The toughness and resiliency of the Afghan tribes served as a reminder of the Sikh Empire's ongoing dangers and external challenges. This insight caused the Sikh ruling class and the larger society to pause and consider the value of effective leadership, the need for military readiness, and the need of defending Sikh interests.

The siege's aftermath had an impact on how the Sikh community saw the larger geopolitical context. The battles made clear how the Sikh Empire, Afghan tribes, and other local entities interacted with one another in terms of power. The difficulties the Sikhs encountered in their efforts to expand into Afghani territory, as well as the results, altered their perception of local politics and the nuances of power conflicts.

The disputes between the Sikhs and the Afghans and their effects on Sikh society also had an influence on how the governing class and the Sikh community interacted. The Sikh Empire, ruled by Maharaja Ranjit Singh and his successors, aimed to retain control over a multiethnic and multireligious populace while consolidating governmental authority. The difficulties presented by the Afghan resistance and the inability to win a resounding victory in battles like the Siege of Jamrud led the Sikh governing class to reflect. This self-examination concentrated on matters of government, military tactics, and the need of striking a balance between Sikh ambitions and the larger interests of the Empire.

Sikh society and culture were significantly impacted by the Siege of Jamrud and other Sikh-Afghan battles. They strengthened Sikh identity and pride, affected military customs, and influenced how the Sikh community saw the balance of power in the area. Reflections on leadership, military readiness, and the difficulties of preserving sovereignty were sparked by the events. These disputes had a profound effect on Sikh society and changed the dynamic between the ruling class and the Sikh populace.

9.2 Historical significance of Nalwa's achievements

It is impossible to overestimate the historical importance of Sardar Hari Singh Nalwa's accomplishments. His military skill, strategic insight, and leadership abilities had a significant influence on the geopolitical environment of the area, the history of the Indian subcontinent, and the Sikh Empire.

The Sikh Empire's boundaries were first and mainly expanded and consolidated under Nalwa. He solidified the Sikh Empire's frontiers via his successful battles and conquests, as well as extending its influence far into the difficult and unstable regions of modern-day Pakistan and Afghanistan. His triumphs in conflicts like the Battle of Jamrud highlighted the Sikh Empire's military might and cemented its dominance over formerly hostile or autonomous territories.

The accomplishments of Nalwa also have important geopolitical ramifications. He upended the established power structures of the area and challenged the authority of opposing forces, such as the Afghan tribes and local kingdoms, by firmly establishing Sikh dominance over significant territory. This altered the regional power structure and had an impact on later political events. The Sikh Empire came into close touch with other powerful nations of the period, such the British East India Company, as a result of Nalwa's conquests, which resulted in complicated relations and confrontations.

Furthermore, the Sikh Army was considerably upgraded by Nalwa's organizational and operational advancements. He built a disciplined and very effective combat force, as well as innovative training techniques and superior weapons. Nalwa's focus on loyalty, discipline, and professionalism gave the Sikh army a strong feeling of unity and pride, making it a powerful combat force. In addition to helping the empire achieve military victories, this upgrading of the Sikh Army had a long-lasting influence on the following development of military tactics and plans in the area.

The accomplishments of Nalwa also had a cultural effect on Sikh culture. His heroic deeds and adventures helped add to the rich fabric of Sikh history and mythology. He became a beloved figure in Sikh culture as a result of his leadership abilities, loyalty to Sikh beliefs, and concern for the welfare of the Sikh community. Even today, Nalwa's bravery and military heritage serve as an inspiration and influence on Sikh identity and pride.

Furthermore, Nalwa's exploits marked an important period in the history of the Indian subcontinent as a whole. His expeditions and successes took place at a period when regional powers fought for dominance and the once-dominant Mughal Empire was in decline. Nalwa's victories demonstrated the rise of a new force, the Sikh Empire, which overthrew the status quo and altered the political and military environment of the area.

The historical importance of Sardar Hari Singh Nalwa's accomplishments resides in his crucial contribution to the enlargement and consolidation of the Sikh Empire's territory, the transformation of the geopolitical environment, the modernization of the Sikh Army, and the imprint he left on Sikh identity and culture. His military accomplishments and leadership skills have made him one of the most renowned and important individuals in Sikh history and have had a significant impact on the history of the Indian subcontinent as a whole.

9.3 Commemoration and remembrance of Sardar Hari Singh Nalwa

Sardar Hari Singh Nalwa's memorialization and remembering are very significant inside and outside of Sikh community. Nalwa is regarded as a renowned character in Sikh history because of his outstanding accomplishments, bravery, and leadership. His legacy is still remembered and honored in a variety of ways.

The creation of monuments and memorials honoring Nalwa's legacy is one of the main ways he is remembered. The Hari Singh Nalwa Memorial, which was created in Gujranwala, Pakistan, to recognize his services to the Sikh

Empire, is the most significant of them. Visitors from all around the globe who want to honor this renowned warrior are drawn to this monument as a source of pride and remembering.

Nalwa is commemorated in Sikh communities via a variety of cultural and religious traditions in addition to physical monuments. Through martial arts performances called Gatka, which highlight the ancient Sikh combat methods that Nalwa and his army were renowned for, his bravery and leadership abilities are often honored. These exhibits preserve and transmit the Sikhs' martial tradition in addition to acting as a reminder of Nalwa's military strength.

Through Sikh religious events like Nagar Kirtans (religious processions), where his name and achievements are often recalled, Nalwa's legacy is also preserved. His identity and accomplishments are preserved through being told to the next generation via oral traditions, Sikh texts, and historical sources.

Additionally, Nalwa's legacy is not limited to the Sikh community. He is a person of importance to historians, academics, and military history enthusiasts because of his accomplishments and the effect he had on the history of the area. Those who are interested in unraveling the complexity of the time continue to study and respect his strategic prowess, military inventions, and the difficulties he encountered in the harsh frontier areas.

The memory of Nalwa is also a source of encouragement for those looking for direction and fortitude in their own life. His unshakable will, leadership abilities, and dedication to his community provide timeless teachings that apply to individuals from all walks of life.

Sardar Hari Singh Nalwa's memorial and memory are essential for maintaining Sikh history, culture, and ideals. Physical monuments, demonstrations of martial arts, religious rituals, and the passing down of his narrative through the generations all serve to respect his legacy. By preserving his legacy, Sikhs and anyone who respect Nalwa's accomplishments may continue to be inspired by his illustrious life and contributions to the Sikh Empire.

Chapter 10

Afghanistan's Resistance against Superpowers

10.1 Overview of Afghanistan's historical resistance

Afghanistan has a long and illustrious history of defending itself against invasion and domination by other powers. The Afghan people have always shown their tenacity and will to preserve their independence and sovereignty. This historical resistance has a long history that spans many wars and fights.

During Alexander the Great's invasion in the fourth century BCE, Afghan resistance was one of the first examples of it that has been documented. The Afghans strongly fought and successfully defended their area despite the huge Macedonian force. This early act of disobedience paved the way for more resistance against foreign forces in the future.

During the 19th century, Afghanistan saw invasions from strong empires looking to increase their influence in the area. Both the First Anglo-Afghan War (1839–1842) and the Second Anglo-Afghan War (1878–1880) saw legendary Afghan resistance. Under the leadership of national heroes like Ahmad Shah Durrani and Sher Ali Khan, the Afghan people engaged in intense combat with the British soldiers, suffering significant casualties and finally forcing the invaders to retreat.

During the Soviet occupation of Afghanistan from 1979 to 1989, there was yet another important instance of resistance. The Mujahideen, or Afghan resistance, waged a clandestine conflict with Soviet soldiers. With the assistance of foreign friends, the Mujahideen used hit-and-run tactics, took advantage of the terrain's mountains, and maintained a strong feeling of patriotic zeal. Their resistance was crucial in loosening the Soviet Union's hold on Afghanistan and ultimately prompted their departure.

The Taliban, an extremist organization that first emerged in the 1990s, have posed problems to Afghanistan in more recent times. Following the Taliban's ascent to power, Afghanistan saw a period of brutal governance and opposition from many groups. After the U.S.-led invasion in 2001, the Taliban administration was finally overthrown thanks in large part to the Northern Alliance, a group of Afghan opposition fighters.

The Afghan people's longstanding feeling of independence, patriotism, and determination to preserving their country are reflected in their historical resistance. Afghanistan's difficult-to-navigate hilly and rocky terrain has created a natural edge for guerrilla warfare and helped the Afghan resistance to fight off more strong invaders with success.

Additionally, the ethnic and tribal variety of Afghanistan is linked to its history of resistance. The Afghan people have historically been divided into tribal groupings, each of which has a distinct identity and a long history of territorial defense. As a result of their ability to organize and oppose foreign invaders on the basis of their common cultural, ethnic, and tribal connections, local communities were able to resist the foreign occupiers, which has contributed to the tenacity of the Afghan resistance.

Afghanistan's continual history of resistance serves as a reminder of the Afghan people's will to defend their independence and preserve their way of life. It also highlights the difficulties that any outside force seeking to impose its will on this historically rebellious country would confront. Afghanistan's perseverance has come to represent the country's identity and the resilient character of its people.

10.2 The Soviet invasion and the Afghan resistance

The Soviet invasion of Afghanistan in 1979 opened a crucial chapter in the country's history and was followed by a protracted period of Afghan resistance. The Soviet Union's determination to assert authority over Afghanistan and back a communist government that had been installed as the consequence of a coup led to the invasion. However, a number of Afghan groups fiercely opposed the invasion, sparking the creation of the Afghan resistance movement.

The Mujahideen, sometimes referred to as the Afghan resistance, was a broad alliance of organizations that opposed the Soviet occupation. Tribal chiefs, religious leaders, thinkers, and combatants from many ethnic groups made up the Mujahideen. Afghan society, which was firmly based on Islamic and tribal customs, supported them.

In order to defeat the much powerful Soviet military, the resistance organization used guerrilla warfare techniques. The Mujahideen used hit-and-run tactics, ambushes, and sabotage to thwart Soviet operations by taking advantage of the challenging Afghan terrain. They received aid from outside parties, such as the United States, Pakistan, Saudi Arabia, and other Arab countries, who gave the Mujahideen weaponry, training, and financial support.

The resistance movement faced certain difficulties. To put down the uprising, the Soviet Union sent out a sizable army and used severe methods. To hinder the Mujahideen's activities, they bombed from the air, carried out retaliation strikes against civilians, and planted minefields. The Mujahideen persisted in fighting despite these obstacles, finding motivation in their steadfast opposition to Western occupation.

The Soviet invasion and Afghan resistance led to a long-lasting and expensive war. Massive misery, enormous loss of life, and extensive displacement were all experienced by the Afghan people. The movement of resistance grew to represent Afghan nationalism and defiance of foreign invasion. As they strove to protect their nation and uphold their way of life, the resistance fighters, also known as freedom fighters, acquired popularity and support among the Afghan populace.

The Soviet Union's occupation of Afghanistan turned out to be a mess that depleted its resources and hurt its standing abroad. The Mujahideen's perseverance and outside assistance finally made the Soviet occupation of Afghanistan more vulnerable. In 1989, the Soviet Union declared its departure in the face of increasing political resistance and fatalities.

The Afghan resistance's battle to stop the Soviet invasion had a significant impact. The fighting sparked the growth of militant beliefs in the area, drew foreign combatants, and energized radical Islamist groups. After the Soviets left, Afghanistan experienced a power vacuum and internal strife, which finally opened the path for the Taliban's ascent.

Afghan history was significantly influenced by both the Soviet invasion and the Afghan resistance. The resistance warriors proved their tenacity, tenacity, and readiness to make sacrifices for the freedom of their homeland. The war had a long-lasting effect on Afghanistan, affecting regional dynamics, its political dynamics, and the country's continuing problems and troubles.

10.3 The US-led invasion and the ongoing conflict

The US-led invasion of Afghanistan in 2001 opened a new crucial chapter in the history of the nation and sparked a protracted struggle that is still influencing the course of the country. The invasion was a direct reaction to the September 11 attacks, which were planned by Al-Qaeda, a terrorist organization that was at the time operating in Afghanistan with the support of the Taliban government.

The main goal of the US-led invasion was to destroy Al-Qaeda and overthrow the Taliban in order to stop Afghanistan from turning into a refuge for terrorists. As a coalition of foreign troops, mostly headed by the United States, used airstrikes and ground operations to erode

Taliban power during the early phase of the invasion, the Taliban administration was quickly overthrown.

After the first military victory, focus switched to stabilizing and reconstructing Afghanistan. A new stage of the war was marked by counterinsurgency operations against a Taliban insurgency that was becoming more and more durable. The insurgency mounted a persistent fight against the Afghan government and foreign troops by capitalizing on grievances, tribal dynamics, and the challenging terrain.

The battle has grown into a drawn-out and complicated confrontation over time. With the assistance of foreign troops, the Afghan government has struggled to build efficient administration, fight corruption, and provide the populace with security and basic amenities. While the battle has intensified and resulted in a high degree of bloodshed and instability, the Taliban, on the other hand, have been able to reorganize and retake control over substantial portions of the nation.

There have been several civilian fatalities as a result of the continuing violence, as well as internal displacement and the degradation of fundamental rights and liberties. The battle has taken a heavy toll on the Afghan people, who have seen people killed, buildings destroyed, and their way of life disrupted. Along with the spread of extremist ideology and cross-border terrorist activity, the war has also led to regional instability.

Political dialogues, peace initiatives, and efforts at reconciliation between the Afghan government and the Taliban have all been part of international efforts to end the war. These initiatives have met with different degrees of success and have encountered many obstacles, such as conflicting interests, ingrained distrust, and the complexity of the political environment in Afghanistan.

The socio-political structure, economics, and security of Afghanistan have all been significantly impacted by the US-led invasion and the protracted struggle that followed. It has put the Afghan people's resiliency to the test and shown the difficulties in establishing stability and lasting peace in a highly fractured and varied nation.

The future of Afghanistan depends on continued work on inclusive government, a negotiated solution, and long-term prosperity. Finding a way to an Afghanistan free from the plague of violence and extremism is still a challenge for the international community, regional players, and the Afghan people themselves.

Chapter 11

USA and USSR: Challenges Faced in Afghanistan

11.1 Brief history of the USA and USSR involvement in Afghanistan

The Soviet Union and the United States' engagement in Afghanistan throughout the 20th century had a profound impact on the history of the nation and the continuing hostilities there.

Beginning in 1979, when they sent armed troops to back a communist government that had been overthrown, the Soviet Union became involved in Afghanistan. The Soviet Union wanted to keep its hold on the area and stabilize the Afghan government. However, other Afghan forces who opposed foreign occupation greeted their involvement with fierce resistance.

The Mujahideen, or Afghan resistance, waged a clandestine conflict with Soviet soldiers. The Mujahideen received assistance from outside parties, particularly the United States, which saw a chance to bolster anti-communist groups and fight Soviet hegemony. Along with other nations like Pakistan and Saudi Arabia, the United States gave the Mujahideen financial support, training, and weaponry.

A lengthy and expensive war with massive casualties and extensive devastation resulted from the conflict's escalation. The Soviet Union decided to withdraw its soldiers in 1989 as a result of rising public opposition to the war and escalating civilian losses. The Soviet Union suffered a great deal as a result of the retreat, which had a lasting effect on the trajectory of the Cold War.

Even after the Soviets left Afghanistan, the United States kept fighting there. Afghanistan fell into a state of civil conflict and political instability in the 1990s, with several groups competing for control. During this time, an extreme group called the Taliban rose to power and took over a large portion of the nation, imposing a strict version of Islamic law.

The United States began a military operation in Afghanistan after the September 11 attacks in 2001, which were planned by the terrorist organization Al-Qaeda operating under Taliban protection. As the Taliban had refused to turn up the terrorist group's leaders, the main goal was to destroy Al-Qaeda and overthrow the government.

The Taliban rule was swiftly overthrown by the US-led invasion, which also installed a new Afghan government. International soldiers continued to operate in Afghanistan as part of the NATO alliance to support the Afghan government, maintain security, and help with the nation's reconstruction.

The Taliban, however, gained momentum and retook control of major portions of the nation as the fight turned into a prolonged insurgency. Along with its foreign partners, the United States has continued to be active in Afghanistan, carrying out counterinsurgency operations and assisting Afghan security forces.

Both the Soviet Union and the United States' engagement in Afghanistan has had profound effects on both the nation and the surrounding area. It is a factor in the continuous hostilities, the spread of extremist beliefs, and the instability of the area. The operations bring to light the difficulties of foreign participation in Afghanistan as well as the difficulties of establishing stability and a lasting peace in a very unstable environment.

During the Cold War, the Soviet Union's engagement in Afghanistan was a component of a larger geopolitical plan. In order to protect itself from possible challenges from the Muslim-majority nations in Central Asia, the Soviet leadership desired to retain a friendly communist government in Afghanistan out of concern about the growth of Islamic extremism. The Afghan people, who saw the Soviet invasion as a danger to their way of life and a violation of their sovereignty, put up a tremendous fight against the invasion.

The Soviet invasion was seen by the United States as a chance to counter Soviet hegemony in the area and back the Afghan resistance. The United States gave the Mujahideen substantial assistance, including weapons, training, and financial support, under the CIA's Operation Cyclone. To direct the aid to the Afghan resistance forces, the CIA collaborated closely with Pakistan's Inter-Services Intelligence (ISI).

The Afghan resistance was seen by the United States and its allies as freedom warriors against a communist invasion. They saw the struggle as a proxy war waged against the Soviet Union with the intention of sapping its resources and hemorrhaging its economy. Additionally, the US sought to stop the Soviet Union from using Afghanistan as a base of operations and a possible starting point for invasion against other nations.

Afghanistan turned into a Cold War battlefield while under Soviet rule. International engagement and attention were drawn to the battle, with different nations backing either the Soviet Union and the Afghan government or the United States and the Afghan resistance. The conflict produced a frontline of proxy combat where the superpowers met one another covertly.

Armed with guerrilla warfare tactics including hit-and-run assaults, ambushes, and improvised explosive devices (IEDs), the Afghan resistance, supported by the international community, caused significant deaths among the Soviet soldiers. The Soviet Union withdrew its soldiers in 1989 as a result of the Mujahideen's tenacity and fortitude as well as growing problems in retaining authority.

Afghanistan was destroyed by the Soviet invasion and subsequent retreat. The nation experienced social disintegration, economic instability, and political fragmentation. The departure left a power vacuum, which led to a civil war and the emergence of several groups vying for dominance. Islamist group the Taliban rose to prominence and finally took control, enforcing a harsh interpretation of Islamic law and providing sanctuary to terrorist groups like Al-Qaeda.

The September 11 attacks led to American engagement in Afghanistan in the 2000s. The US-led invasion sought to destroy Al-Qaeda and overthrow the Taliban because it believed they were involved in giving the terrorist organization refuge. Although the US-led coalition initially had military victory against the Taliban rule, stabilizing the nation and building efficient administration proved difficult.

Afghanistan's continuous battle has proven to be a difficult and drawn-out operation. The war has continued despite major efforts and funding from the international community, especially the United States, NATO, and other allies. The Taliban insurgency has persisted, and there have been many challenges in the way of attempts to create a stable, democratic Afghanistan.

Afghanistan and the surrounding area have been negatively impacted by the USSR and USA's presence there. The spread of weaponry, the radicalization of certain Afghan societal segments, and the eviction of millions of people are all results of it. Additionally, the war has strained ties between regional powers, heightened ethnic and sectarian violence, and had a significant negative humanitarian impact.

The history of US and USSR engagement in Afghanistan highlights the difficulties in attaining long-term security in a nation with entrenched tribal, ethnic, and ideological differences as well as the complexity of foreign operations. It serves as a reminder of the long-lasting effects of geopolitical rivalry and the significance of all-encompassing strategies for tackling the many problems Afghanistan and its people confront.

When they were each involved in Afghanistan, the Soviet Union and the United States used various plans and techniques. In order to crush the Afghan resistance, the Soviet Union relied on traditional military might, sending out a sizable contingent of soldiers and powerful weapons. They built up a network of military outposts and made an effort to maintain control over important transportation hubs and metropolitan areas. However, their methods often alienated the Afghan people and stoked further opposition.

In contrast, the United States supported the Afghan resistance in a more covert manner. They supported the Mujahideen financially, militarily, and logistically, mostly by supplying them with equipment and providing training. The CIA and ISI collaborated extensively to provide help to the resistance forces, allowing them to successfully execute their guerrilla warfare strategies. The US assistance was centered on strengthening regional Afghan factions and taking advantage of the Soviet Union's weaknesses.

The engagement of the USA and USSR in Afghanistan has enormous regional effects. The dispute evolved into a bigger regional power struggle in which the surrounding nations each played a part. Particularly important to the Mujahideen and receiving significant US backing was Pakistan. Iran, on the other hand, backed several Afghan forces while attempting to counterbalance Soviet influence.

The battle heightened tensions between regional powers and stoked rivalries among their proxies.

Beyond Afghan boundaries, the effects of US and USSR participation in Afghanistan were felt. International jihadist militants who saw the resistance as a holy war against the Soviet Union were drawn to the fighting. Some of these foreign warriors, like Osama bin Laden, rose to notoriety and formed international terrorist organizations, which had long-lasting effects on world security.

The limitations of military intervention and the difficulties of nation-building were also made clear by the USSR and US participation in Afghanistan. The complexity of Afghan culture, particularly its tribal dynamics, ethnic differences, and deeply ingrained adherence to regional traditions and customs, were underappreciated by both superpowers. Long-term instability was compounded by the operations' frequent disruption of local power structures and escalation of already-expressed concerns.

The USA and USSR's engagement in Afghanistan also showed the military's limits in bringing about long-term political solutions. Despite the Mujahideen's military victories and the Soviet Union's ultimate exit, the nation continued to experience unrest and instability. The many Afghan groups' internal power struggles, division, and conflicting interests hindered attempts at reconciliation and the development of a stable administration.

The United States and the Soviet Union's participation in Afghanistan also demonstrated the limits of immediate geopolitical considerations. Initially, neither superpower fully considered the long-term repercussions as they pursued their strategic goals. Future regional stability will face enormous obstacles as a result of the instability caused by the Soviet exit and the following power conflicts, which allowed extremist organizations to thrive.

Significant historical, regional, and international repercussions resulted from the USSR and USA's engagement in Afghanistan. The battle brought to light the difficulties of foreign interventions, the limitations of military force, and the difficulties of forming a country in a pluralistic and fractured society. It sparked geopolitical rivalries, influenced the emergence of international terrorism, and had a long-lasting effect on Afghanistan and the surrounding area. The approaches to foreign intervention and conflict resolution attempts in Afghanistan and elsewhere continue to be shaped by the lessons learnt from past initiatives.

11.2 Motivations and objectives of both superpowers

During the Cold War, the geopolitical interests of the Soviet Union and the United States guided their engagement in Afghanistan and served as their reasons. As part of a larger plan to increase and strengthen Soviet influence in the area, the Soviet Union's major aim was to establish and sustain a favorable communist government in Afghanistan. They sought to install a socialist government that adhered to their ideological ideas and acted as a defense against prospective challenges from Central Asian nations with a majority of Muslims.

A second goal of the Soviet Union was to stop the growth of Islamic extremism and any prospective Islamic revolution that would influence Muslim communities both within and outside of its borders. Afghanistan was an important country for the Soviet Union to exercise influence and maintain control over the region because of its strategic position bordering Iran and Pakistan.

In addition, the Soviet Union saw the Afghan crisis as a chance to extend its military might and assert its superiority as a superpower on a worldwide scale. In the context of the larger Cold War competition, the intervention was considered as a method for the Soviet Union to demonstrate its capabilities and counteract American influence.

On the other side, the Soviet participation in Afghanistan was seen by the United States as a chance to restrain Soviet growth and influence in the area. They were worried that Afghanistan may end up as a Soviet bastion and a starting point for further Soviet agression in the Middle East and South Asia.

Additionally, the United States had a stake in halting the development of communism and assisting anti-communist movements across the world. Due of the Soviet Union's involvement, the United States had the chance to aid the Afghan resistance, which was seen as a proxy army defending against a communist invasion. The United States wanted to undermine the Soviet Union and deplete its resources in order to win the Cold War, thus it sent assistance, weapons, and training to the Afghan resistance fighters.

Additionally, the United States saw the Afghan war as a chance to strengthen its regional strategic position. Afghanistan was a crucial region of interest for the United

States due to its closeness to oil-rich nations in the Persian Gulf and its strategic placement close to vital trade routes. The United States' participation in Afghanistan gave it the chance to influence the area and defend its larger geopolitical and economic interests.

The Soviet Union's objectives in Afghanistan were to increase its power, uphold a friendly government, and halt the growth of Islamic extremism. On the other side, the United States sought to thwart Soviet expansion, aid anti-communist movements, and defend its own economic and geopolitical interests in the area. In the framework of the larger Cold War competition, the fighting in Afghanistan became into a battlefield where the superpowers pursued their geopolitical goals.

11.3 Military strategies and setbacks faced by the USA and USSR

During their different involvements in Afghanistan, the Soviet Union and the United States each encountered distinct military difficulties and defeats. Following its participation in 1979, the Soviet Union originally used a traditional military approach. To impose authority over important metropolitan areas and transportation hubs, they sent out a sizable army with powerful weapons. By using conventional warfare, the Soviet troops sought to defeat the Mujahideen, or Afghan resistance, and install a powerful, Moscow-aligned government. However, they encountered a number of severe obstacles.

The rocky, hilly terrain of Afghanistan was one of the main challenges the Soviet soldiers faced. The topography made it difficult for the Soviets to successfully counter the

Mujahideen's use of guerilla warfare. Because they were acquainted with the surrounding terrain, the resistance fighters used hit-and-run strategies, ambushes, and unconventional warfare to elude and confront the Soviet troops.

Afghan resistance was tenacious and very motivated, which the Soviet soldiers also encountered. The Mujahideen warriors were fiercely dedicated to protecting their nation against what they saw as an invasion by foreigners. They took advantage of the Soviet Union's weak points in logistics by sabotaging supply routes and communication connections. A major defeat for the Soviet troops was the Mujahideen's ability to wage a prolonged guerrilla war against a technologically superior foe.

In addition, the Soviet Union had to deal with increasing war-related deaths and internal resistance. The war lost support among the populace of the Soviet Union as many people questioned the benefits and rationale for their participation in a far-off, apparently hopeless fight. The Soviet Union decided to withdraw its soldiers in 1989 as a result of the conflict's heavy human and financial costs, which put a burden on its resources.

In a similar vein, when it came to its military participation in Afghanistan, the United States also faced considerable difficulties and defeats. Although the Taliban government was overthrown by the first US-led invasion in 2001, the character of the battle changed in the years that followed. The Taliban insurgency and other extremist organizations forced the United States and its allies to fight a drawn-out and difficult war.

The difficulties of conducting an asymmetrical war against a dispersed and adaptable adversary was one of the biggest problems for the US military. Guerilla tactics were used by the Taliban and other rebel organizations to sneak enter towns and carry out random assaults. Because of this, it was difficult for the US military to recognize and successfully combat its enemies.

The US military was also tasked with the difficult job of stabilizing and nation-building a war-torn nation. Rebuilding infrastructure, ensuring security, and establishing efficient governing institutions all proven to be difficult tasks. The establishment of a stable and functional administration was made difficult by the convoluted sociopolitical dynamics, corruption, and the involvement of local power brokers.

The protracted struggle also placed a heavy burden on US military capabilities and popular support. The morale and wellbeing of US soldiers were affected by the protracted deployments and high fatality rates. Public support for the protracted presence in Afghanistan decreased as a result of the financial expenses of the war, which also had an impact on the US economy and domestic priorities.

In Afghanistan, the Soviet Union and the United States both suffered military failures that brought to light the challenges of battling a motivated foe in a challenging environment. The lessons learned by both superpowers highlighted the limits of military might in forging long-lasting political agreements as well as the difficulties of nation-building in a sharply divided and fractured society.

One of the biggest defeats for the Soviet Union was the flexibility and tenacity of the Afghan resistance. Despite suffering severe casualties, the Mujahideen forces, who were made up of many Afghan groups, showed an extraordinary capacity to rebuild and go on with their battle. They took advantage of the Soviet Union's flaws and modified their strategies to combat the Soviet troops' overwhelming weaponry. The Mujahideen made it difficult for the Soviet troops to establish a clear advantage by using improvised explosive devices (IEDs), guerilla tactics, and local terrain expertise.

In order to win the Afghan people's hearts and minds, the Soviet Union also had to overcome obstacles. Due to indiscriminate bombings, forced relocations, and violations of human rights, the Soviet strategy often resulted in the alienation of the local populace. As a result, the Mujahideen were able to pose themselves as protectors of Afghan sovereignty and Islam against a foreign invader, which provided a favorable environment for their recruitment and support. The Soviet-backed regime's lack of public support made its military operations ineffective.

In terms of military tactics, the Soviet Union made an effort to control important metropolitan centres and main thoroughfares, deploying soldiers to important cities including Kabul, Kandahar, and Herat. They aimed to bolster their hold on major metropolitan areas and sabotage the Mujahideen's supply routes. To successfully govern the wide rural territories and isolated places where the resistance fighters operated, the Soviet troops, however, had difficulties.

During its engagement in Afghanistan, the United States encountered a unique set of military difficulties. Conventional warfare dominated the early stages of the US-led invasion in 2001, which had the objectives of overthrowing the Taliban government and destroying Al-Qaeda. Precision airstrikes, special forces operations, and the use of conventional ground forces were the main priorities.

However, as the fight progressed, the US military was forced to modify its tactics to deal with a Taliban insurgency that was becoming more dispersed and tenacious. The militants used asymmetric warfare strategies like as hit-and-run operations, roadside bombs, suicide strikes, and others. The battle became more difficult as a result of the Taliban's ability to blend in with the local populace and take advantage of the permeable border with Pakistan.

The US military also had to manage counterinsurgency operations and nation-building initiatives at the same time. A stable Afghan government, security, and infrastructure reconstruction were the goals. These attempts faced major obstacles because of the complexity of Afghan culture, the presence of regional power brokers, and a lack of institutional ability.

The emergence of new extremist organizations like the Islamic State (ISIS) in Afghanistan was another setback for the US. The rise of these organizations complicated the battle further and put further pressure on the coalition headed by the US.

Furthermore, logistical and supply-line issues were a problem for both the Soviet Union and the United States. Logistics challenges were caused by the hostile terrain, a lack of infrastructure, and the necessity to move soldiers, supplies, and equipment across great distances. Both times, keeping a steady and trustworthy supply chain proved to be quite difficult.

Summary: During their separate involvements in Afghanistan, the Soviet Union and the United States suffered a number of military defeats. By taking advantage of the flaws in the methods and tactics of the superpowers, the Afghan resistance showed tenacity and flexibility. The Soviet Union and the United States both had problems because to the rough terrain, the enemy's dispersed character, the lack of public support, and logistical issues. These failures brought to light the difficulties of fighting in a harsh and politically fractured setting and underlined the limits of military might in bringing about long-term stability and victory.

The problem of insurgency and asymmetrical warfare was one of the major defeats for the Soviet Union. The Mujahideen, or Afghan resistance fighters, were adept at adjusting to Soviet strategies and taking advantage of their flaws. They attacked weak Soviet convoys and supply routes with hit-and-run operations and ambushes. Because the Mujahideen militants could blend in with the local populace, it was difficult for the Soviet troops to tell who was a friend and who was an enemy and to put down the rebellion.

The Soviet Union also faced difficulties because to the tenacity and outside backing given to the Afghan resistance. The United States, Saudi Arabia, and other nations gave the Mujahideen a lot of assistance. The Mujahideen were able to continue their battle against the Soviet troops because to this help, which included weapons, training, and financial resources.

It was challenging for the Soviet Union to gain the Afghan people's allegiance and confidence. The Soviet military's oppressive methods, including as indiscriminate bombings and violations of human rights, alienated the local populace and stoked anti-Soviet feelings. Establishing a legal and functioning administration that could win the public's support was difficult for the Soviet troops.

On the other side, the United States had its own difficulties while participating in the Afghan war. Once the Taliban administration had been overthrown, the US-led coalition concentrated on stabilizing the nation and establishing an effective Afghan government. However, their attempts were significantly hampered by the complicated social and political dynamics, pervasive corruption, and other factors.

The US forces also had to deal with insurgency, notably with the Taliban's comeback. To gather support and retake power in certain places, the Taliban took advantage of locals' complaints about things like a lack of employment prospects and poor government. They regrouped and launched operations against the US and Afghan troops using guerrilla tactics and safe havens in neighboring Pakistan.

The US also struggled to strike a balance between military goals and the necessity to protect civilians while limiting collateral damage. It was difficult to carry out military operations without running the danger of harming civilians due to the asymmetrical nature of the fight and the presence of militants among the civilian population.

For the United States, logistical difficulties were a factor, especially in maintaining a sizable military presence in a landlocked nation with poor infrastructure. Long distances and sometimes difficult terrain had to be traversed in order to move soldiers, equipment, and supplies, which created logistical challenges and risks.

During their involvements in Afghanistan, the Soviet Union and the United States both encountered substantial military difficulties and failures. The complexity and frustration of the superpowers' military operations were exacerbated by insurgent tactics, outside help for the resistance, difficulty in obtaining public support, and logistical limitations. These encounters brought home how tough the Afghan opposition is, how complicated the local dynamics are, and how difficult it is to carry out successful military operations abroad.

Chapter 12

A Comparison of Nalwa's Victories with Superpowers

12.1 Analyzing the scale and context of Nalwa's victories

Sardar Hari Singh Nalwa's triumphs were noteworthy in both scope and context, and they had broad repercussions for the area. The military accomplishments of Nalwa proved the superior leadership abilities, strategic thinking, and efficiency of the Sikh Army under his command.

Scale-wise, Nalwa's triumphs stood out for their size and significance. He oversaw many successful operations against Afghan armies that resulted in the expansion of the Sikh Empire's realms and Sikh dominance over sizable areas. With the help of Nalwa, the Sikh Empire's frontiers were expanded into the northwest frontier regions, including Peshawar, Attock, and Jamrud, which were formerly regarded as bastions of Afghan authority.

Nalwa's triumphs were notable in part because of the situation they took place in. In the context of an Afghan monarchy that had previously shown resistance to foreign invasions, he accomplished these victories. Afghanistan has resisted several efforts to be subjugated by strong empires like the British, Persian, and Mughal. Nalwa and the Sikh Army's ability to beat Afghan forces—who had previously been repulsed by powerful international powers—is evidence of their superior military skills.

Nalwa's wins were not singular events; rather, they were a component of a larger strategic plan. He was aware of the northwest frontier's geopolitical significance and understood how crucial it was to protect these areas for the Sikh Empire. For the purpose of strengthening Sikh dominance and defending the recently conquered regions against Afghan counterattacks, Nalwa strategically placed Sikh garrisons and forts in key sites.

Furthermore, the area now enjoys stability and security because to Nalwa's triumphs. He put policies in place to secure the safety of the local populace, supported trade and business, and promoted the development of infrastructure and agriculture. These initiatives promoted stability and Sikh influence in the area and helped to the general prosperity and growth of the recently gained regions.

Beyond mere territorial conquest, Nalwa's triumphs are significant. His achievements had significant political ramifications and illustrated the might and prowess of the Sikh Empire under Maharaja Ranjit Singh. The Sikh Empire's status as a regional power was cemented by Nalwa's successes, which also made obvious the Sikh military strength to other nations.

Furthermore, Nalwa's accomplishments had a long-lasting influence on the region's historical development. The nations he conquered were permanently incorporated into the Sikh Empire and had a significant impact on its growth and reach. The local culture, government, and governance structures have been forever influenced by the Sikh reign in these regions.

Sardar Singh Hari Nalwa's wins were noteworthy due to the scope and setting of them. His military victories against Afghan armies increased the Sikh Empire's realms and strengthened Sikh authority in difficult historical contexts. Nalwa's victories demonstrated his capacity for leadership, his capacity for strategic thinking, and the might of the Sikh Army. These victories had far-reaching effects on the region's history as well as geopolitical relevance, political stability, and other factors.

12.2 Comparing the strategies and military capabilities of the superpowers and Nalwa

The superpowers, notably the USA and USSR, had very different military capacities and plans than Sardar Hari Singh Nalwa. Nalwa used a mix of creative methods, tactical genius, and a profound grasp of the local geography and culture while the superpowers relied on traditional military techniques and overwhelming weapons.

The superpowers, in particular the USSR, mainly depended on their superior technical capabilities and the use of sizable conventional armies. They consolidated control and superiority on the battlefield by using powerful air support, armored divisions, and artillery barrages. To seize control of important metropolitan centres and eradicate resistance fighters, the USSR used a "search and destroy" tactic. However, the dispersed and adaptable character of the Afghan resistance meant that their dependence on conventional warfare tactics was less successful.

Nalwa, on the other hand, was aware of the limits of conventional combat in Afghanistan's difficult terrain. He emphasized guerilla warfare, close quarters combat, and hit-and-run operations, which enabled his troops to take advantage of the Afghan forces' vulnerabilities and do maximum damage with the least amount of resources. Because of their excellent mobility and skill in negotiating the difficult terrain, Nalwa's soldiers were able to ambush and surprise the enemy.

Nalwa also showed that she had a solid grasp of the value of intelligence and reconnaissance. He developed a network of informers and spies, which gave him vital knowledge on the enemy's activities, advantages, and disadvantages. He was able to organize and carry out effective operations with pinpoint accuracy thanks to this intelligence-driven strategy, minimizing unwarranted risks and maximizing the impact of his soldiers.

Nalwa was also renowned for his creative defense tactics and fortification designs. He set up strong defensive lines, reinforced strategic locations, and made use of the terrain's inherent characteristics to build a powerful defense. Due to this, he was able to fend off Afghan offensives and resist enemy assaults while being outnumbered. Nalwa's knowledge of defensive warfare and his talent for using the defensive advantages provided by the terrain were shown by his ability to hold key locations for protracted periods of time.

The superpowers held the advantage in terms of military prowess because to their abundant resources, cutting-edge weapons, and logistical support. They had highly developed tanks, artillery, planes, and other sophisticated equipment, giving them a considerable firepower and range. However, the difficult terrain of Afghanistan often nullified the benefits of such cutting-edge weapons, making it difficult for the superpowers to secure resounding triumphs.

In contrast, Nalwa depended on a force that was highly disciplined and motivated, which he trained and outfitted to meet the needs of the environment and the kind of conflict he foresaw. His troops excelled in hit-and-run tactics and close quarters battle, and they were skilled in irregular conflict and mountain warfare. Even though his soldiers were outnumbered and outgunned, Nalwa's focus on individual marksmanship, mobility, and flexibility helped them to outmaneuver and deceive the opposition.

The superpowers' military might and Sardar Hari Singh Nalwa's military tactics were quite different. While Nalwa used cutting-edge tactics, guerilla warfare, and a thorough awareness of the region's geography and culture, the superpowers relied on traditional military techniques, overwhelming weaponry, and technical dominance. With a focus on mobility, intelligence, defensive fortifications, and agility, Nalwa was able to defeat the Afghan troops with surprising success, demonstrating the efficacy of his unorthodox strategy in the difficult environment of Afghanistan.

12.3 Lessons learned from Nalwa's successes

Sardar Singh Hari Nalwa's military victories provide important lessons that may be applied to military tactics and leadership tenets. These are some of the most important lessons drawn from Nalwa's accomplishments:

Nalwa gave a compelling example of the value of adaptation and flexibility in combat. He understood the need of adapting tactics and plans to the terrain, the enemy's capabilities, and the general context of the fight. Nalwa was able to optimize the efficiency of his troops by taking advantage of opportunities, minimizing risks, and responding rapidly to changing conditions.

- Information and Reconnaissance: Nalwa's focus on collecting information and conducting reconnaissance was essential to his success. He was aware of the need of having up-to-date knowledge on the capabilities, vulnerabilities, and objectives of the opposition. Nalwa was able to organize operations efficiently, make educated judgments, and take advantage of holes in the enemy's defenses thanks to the knowledge gathered by informers and spies.

- Guerrilla warfare and asymmetric tactics: Nalwa's adoption of these strategies demonstrated the potency of unorthodox methods in difficult situations. Nalwa increased the effectiveness of his men by using hit-and-run tactics, ambushes, and surprise assaults to throw the opponent off guard. This emphasizes the value of using original thoughts and unconventional techniques to accomplish military goals.

- Fortifications and Defensive techniques: Nalwa's knowledge of fortifications and defensive techniques illustrated the importance of well-designed defenses in securing strategic locations and repelling enemy assaults. He demonstrated the value of using natural topographical characteristics, building strong defensive lines, and exploiting the defensive advantages provided by the environment by his ability to hold crucial areas for lengthy periods of time.

- Leadership and Unity: Nalwa's achievements were credited to both his military prowess and his capacity to inspire teamwork among his soldiers. He inspired his troops to provide their best efforts despite hardship because he commanded their respect and allegiance. In order to accomplish military goals, strong leadership, good communication, and a feeling of purpose among all team members are critical. This is highlighted by Nalwa's leadership style.

- Local Knowledge & Cultural Understanding: Nalwa's success was largely due to his in-depth knowledge of the region's geography, culture, and social structures. Using this information to his advantage, he was able to successfully negotiate the challenging terrain of Afghanistan, form bonds with the tribes there, and win the support of the local populace. This underlines the significance of cultural sensitivity and the capacity to modify military tactics to the particulars of the fight.

- Sustainable Governance and Development: Nalwa's accomplishments went beyond only conquering territory militarily. In the areas he conquered, he understood the value of sustainable government and development. Nalwa concentrated on stimulating infrastructural growth, trade, commerce, agriculture, and stability in the newly annexed areas. This emphasizes how important it is to combine military achievements with initiatives to promote efficient administration and socioeconomic growth.

The significance of adaptation, intelligence, guerilla warfare, defensive methods, strong leadership, cultural understanding, and sustainable government are just a few of the lessons acquired from Sardar Hari Singh Nalwa's victories. These lessons may be applied to modern military tactics, highlighting the necessity for innovative thinking, using local expertise, and maintaining a holistic strategy that takes into account not just military goals but also the welfare and development of the impacted communities.

Chapter 13

The Relevance of Nalwa's Strategies in Modern Warfare

13.1 Applying Nalwa's military tactics in contemporary conflicts

Sardar Singh Hari Military tactics and techniques used by Nalwa may provide important insights and lessons that can be applied to current wars. The following are some ways in which Nalwa's military strategies might be applicable in contemporary conflict, despite the fact that the unique setting and dynamics of each fight may vary:

Flexibility and Adaptability: Modern conflicts often take place in complex and dynamic situations. It's critical to be adaptable in modifying strategy and tactics in response to shifting conditions. Nalwa was able to make wise choices and take advantage of chances because to his rapid ability to react to the surroundings, adversary actions, and the overall situation. Military leaders in contemporary wars must remain adaptable in their strategies, constantly reevaluating and revising their plans as the situation changes.

- Intelligence and Reconnaissance: In a battle, information is a vital tool. Effective decision-making requires accurate and timely information collection regarding the capabilities, intentions, and weaknesses of the opponent. The importance Nalwa placed on information collecting and reconnaissance offers a crucial lesson for modern battles. To get a thorough grasp of the battlefield and make wise operational decisions, modern forces need invest in intelligence capabilities, such as surveillance technology, human intelligence networks, and cyber intelligence.

- Special Operations and Asymmetric Warfare: Asymmetric warfare, in which one side battles a stronger opponent, is becoming more common in contemporary wars. The success of unconventional strategies in such circumstances is shown by Nalwa's employment of guerilla warfare and asymmetric tactics. Special operations troops are capable of carrying out precision attacks, gathering information, and sabotaging enemy activities. They are outfitted with specialized training and equipment. When fighting opponents that possess better technology, incorporating aspects of asymmetric warfare into military plans might provide an important edge.

- Defensive tactics and counterinsurgency: Nalwa's understanding of fortifications and defensive tactics might be useful in today's counterinsurgency operations. Strong defensive positions, safe bases, and counterinsurgency strategies may help defend population centers, safeguard military personnel, and win over local populations' confidence. This strategy may help reduce fatalities, stop insurgent activity, and aid with stability and development operations.

- Cultural awareness and Civil-Military Cooperation: Nalwa's awareness of the value of fostering ties with local people and understanding other cultures is pertinent in today's conflicts marked by insurgencies and counterinsurgencies. Armed forces can handle challenging terrain, win over local populations, and lower the risk of civilian deaths by being aware of the local culture, customs, and social dynamics. Collaboration with local authorities and civilian agencies is a crucial component of civil-military cooperation, which is necessary for building efficient administration, providing needed services, and gaining the support of the populace.

Stabilization and post-conflict rebuilding efforts are essential in today's conflicts, which is why Nalwa focused on sustainable government and development in the lands he controlled. Integrating military operations with long-term development programs may aid in establishing the prerequisites for enduring peace and avert the resumption of conflict. This involves promoting the rule of law, healthcare, education, and infrastructure development.

The basic concepts of adaptation, intelligence, asymmetric warfare, defensive methods, cultural understanding, and sustainable development may be modified to particular circumstances, even though it may not be possible to directly use Nalwa's military tactics in all contemporary conflicts. Modern military commanders may improve their strategy and operations, successfully traverse challenging settings, and support effective attempts at conflict resolution and peacebuilding by learning from the past.

13.2 Adapting Nalwa's leadership principles to modern warfare

Sardar Hari Singh's adaptation Modern military commanders may benefit from the advice that Nalwa's leadership principles for modern warfare can provide. Even if the nature of battle has changed, certain core leadership ideas are still valid. Here are some examples of how Nalwa's leadership ideas might be used in contemporary conflict:

- Lead by Example: Nalwa set a good example, showing restraint, fortitude, and a solid work ethic. Modern military commanders should exhibit the traits they want in their troops. Being physically fit, displaying professionalism and honesty, and taking the initiative may build trust and encourage soldiers to provide their best effort.

- Effective Communication: Nalwa understood the need of precise orders being communicated to his men in order to promote unity. Modern military commanders should place a high priority on timely, clear, and succinct communication in order to successfully transmit goals, expectations, and situational awareness. Operational effectiveness may be increased by embracing contemporary communication technology and preserving an open and transparent communication channel.

- Decision-making and Adaptability: Nalwa's success was largely a result of his ability to adjust to shifting conditions. Modern military commanders need to be adaptable and agile, with the ability to act fast and with knowledge. The capacity to assess complicated circumstances, have a thorough awareness of the operating environment, and be prepared to modify plans and tactics as needed are requirements for this.

- Developing Subordinates: Nalwa developed his subordinates by giving them responsibility and chances to demonstrate their abilities. A culture that values initiative, creativity, and decentralized decision-making should be promoted by modern military commanders. This not only improves the skills of the whole army but also encourages subordinates to take responsibility for their actions.

- Cultural Awareness and Relationship-Building: Nalwa's focus on cultural awareness and relationship-building with locals is pertinent in contemporary combat, especially in counterinsurgency and stability operations. Military officials should fund cultural sensitivity training and exhort their soldiers to interact politely with locals. Building relationships based on mutual respect and trust may promote collaboration for mission success, assist gather crucial information, and reduce possible causes of conflict.

Nalwa's dedication to ethical behavior and respect for human rights serves as a timeless lesson in these concepts. Protection of people, respect to international humanitarian law, and the morale of their personnel must all be prioritized by modern military commanders. Maintaining these values improves credibility, fortifies ties with the community, and promotes long-term stability.

Nalwa showed strategic vision by comprehending the more general goals and making plans for long-term success. Modern military commanders must have a distinct strategic vision that links their choices and actions to larger goals. This entails foreseeing potential obstacles, seeing opportunities, and creating strategies that take diverse possibilities into consideration.

Military commanders may inspire their people, build unity, and successfully manage the difficulties of current wars by applying Nalwa's leadership ideas to modern combat. While respecting moral norms and respect for human rights, incorporating these principles may improve operational effectiveness, streamline coordination with coalition allies and regional stakeholders, and help missions succeed.

13.3 The enduring legacy of Nalwa's strategies

Beyond his own lifetime, Sardar Hari Singh Nalwa's ideas have left a lasting impact that still influences military strategists today. His cutting-edge and effective military strategies have had a profound effect on how warfare is understood and used today. The following are some elements of Nalwa's tactics that have influenced military doctrine:

- Tactical genius: Nalwa's adaptable and flexible ways to combat have been the subject of much study and admiration due to his tactical genius. He demonstrated the value of strategic thought and operational preparation by evaluating the opponent, taking advantage of their vulnerabilities, and using the terrain. Nalwa's tactical innovations are still being studied and used as an inspiration by military academics and strategists in the context of current wars.

- Guerrilla Warfare: Nalwa's successful use of guerrilla warfare techniques in difficult terrain established a standard for unconventional warfare tactics. His ambushes, surprise assaults, and hit-and-run raids served as a model for later guerrilla groups and rebels. Modern practitioners of unconventional warfare have been impacted by Nalwa's legacy in guerilla warfare in terms of strategy and approach.

- Defense Fortifications: Nalwa made significant contributions to military engineering via his knowledge of defensive tactics and fortifications. His ability to fortify key places and form defensive lines demonstrated the value of strengthening powerful fortifications. The design and building of military structures, both in offensive and defensive operations, continue to be influenced by Nalwa's focus on fortifications.

- Integration of Local Knowledge: Nalwa's grasp of the value of cultural familiarity and local knowledge has proven to be a vital lesson for military officers working in foreign situations. The value of incorporating local knowledge and interacting with the communities in which armed personnel operate is shown by his capacity to forge connections with local tribes, manage the complexities of Afghan culture, and capitalize on the support of local people.

Sardar Hari Singh Nalwa's accomplishments have left a lasting impression on Indian military history, and they are revered as a testament to his valor and strategic acumen. His successes against Afghan troops and contributions to the growth of the Sikh Empire have been documented and analyzed, offering important insights into Indian military history and customs. Following generations of Indian military officers have been motivated and inspired to serve their country as a result of Nalwa's legacy.

Inspiration for Leadership: Nalwa continues to be an inspiration for military commanders all over the globe with his leadership abilities and strategic vision. His capacity to inspire loyalty, promote cooperation, and set a positive example highlights the age-old rules of successful leadership. The legacy of Nalwa inspires military commanders to adopt strategic thinking, agility, and moral behavior in their choices and deeds.

The techniques of Sardar Hari Singh Nalwa have endured because they are still relevant and used in modern military doctrine. For military commanders and strategists, his tactical genius, creative approaches to battle, attention on cultural understanding, and successful leadership serve as timeless teachings. The contributions of Nalwa to military history continue to influence how combat is understood and practiced, leaving a permanent imprint on both the art and science of military strategy.

Chapter 14

Historical and Geopolitical Factors in Afghanistan's Resilience

14.1 Understanding Afghanistan's geographical and cultural factors

Afghanistan's history, politics, and socioeconomic dynamics are significantly shaped by its geographical and cultural characteristics. Geographically speaking, the nation is unusual since it is at the nexus of Central, South, and West Asia, which has an impact on its strategic significance and relations with surrounding areas. The following are some significant geographical and cultural elements of Afghanistan:

- Strategic Location: Due to its geographic position, Afghanistan has historically served as a hub for commerce, cultural exchanges, and geopolitical conflict. It acts as a geographical connection between South Asia, Central Asia, and the Middle East, acting as a hub for a number of historical civilizations and trade routes. The nation's geographic position has also left it open to invasions and power conflicts by other empires vying for control over trade routes and regional influence.

- Tribal institutions: The social and political structure of Afghanistan has been significantly influenced by traditional tribal institutions. Tribal alliances and allegiances often cross international borders and may affect the balance of power inside a nation. Understanding and interacting with tribal dynamics is essential for good government and stability in Afghanistan since tribal leaders have traditionally had significant influence over the local populace.

- Nomadic Traditions: of the past, pastoralist populations of Afghanistan, like the Kuchi people, would travel the area with their animals. These nomadic practices have influenced social and economic dynamics as well as how nomadic tribes and established communities interact. Tensions over resources and land have sometimes arisen as a result of encounters between agriculturally established settled populations and nomadic nomads.

- Islamic Influence: Islam is the most common religion in Afghanistan, and Sunni Islam is practiced by the vast majority of the country's citizens. The nation's social standards, legal structures, and cultural practices have been significantly influenced by Islamic traditions and ideals. Islam's effect on tribal and ethnic identities is often intermingled, which adds to the intricate interaction of religious, cultural, and social forces in Afghan culture.

Afghanistan has a hilly, rocky geography, with the Hindu Kush mountain range taking up much of the country's landscape. The country's hilly terrain has traditionally posed difficulties for military operations, making it challenging for outside forces to exercise total authority over the area. The local troops are able to stave off invasions and preserve some degree of autonomy because to the hilly terrain's inherent defensive advantages.

Afghanistan is home to a variety of ethnic and tribal groupings, each of which has its own unique cultural traditions, dialects, and identities. To the nation's cultural fabric, Pashtuns, Tajiks, Hazaras, Uzbeks, and other ethnic groups also contribute. Although it is a source of strength and resilience, this variety has also contributed to ethnic tensions and conflicts inside the nation.

Understanding Afghanistan's physical and cultural characteristics is essential for appreciating the historical setting, political difficulties, and sociological complexity of the nation. In order to navigate its way towards stability, growth, and peace, Afghanistan must contend with a number of unique problems and possibilities due to its harsh terrain, strategic position, ethnic variety, tribal systems, nomadic customs, and Islamic influence.

14.2 The role of tribalism, guerrilla warfare, and local resistance

Afghanistan's history has been significantly shaped by tribalism, guerrilla warfare, and local resistance, especially in the face of foreign invasions and efforts at centralized rule. These elements have had a significant influence on the nation's political dynamics, military tactics, and populace resiliency.

Tribalism: Tribal ties and institutions have long shaped Afghanistan's social and political climate. The nation is home to a number of different ethnic and tribal groupings, each of which has its own unique cultural traditions, allegiances, and power structures. Tribal chiefs are powerful figures in their communities, and their support or opposition may affect the course of politics. Tribal networks have often provided crucial sources of mobilization, resistance, and protection during times of conflict or outside attack. Tribal dynamics are crucial to Afghan culture and politics since devotion to one's tribe might trump allegiance to a governing body.

Guerilla Warfare: Afghanistan has a history of fighting foreign invaders using guerilla tactics. The nation's difficult geography, which includes hilly areas and extensive cave systems, offers guerilla warfare inherent benefits. To combat superior enemy troops, Afghan fighters have used hit-and-run tactics, ambushes, and asymmetrical warfare. Smaller, dispersed units may use their terrain expertise, blend in with the community, and mount a sustained defense using this kind of warfare. Afghan soldiers have always been able to resist and exhaust bigger, conventional armies by using guerilla warfare effectively.

Local Resistance: In defending Afghan land and claiming independence from foreign forces, local resistance organizations have been crucial. Afghans have vehemently opposed invasions, often rising up against the invading armies. Afghans have a strong feeling of identity and togetherness due to their commitment to defend their country and oppose foreign occupation. In order to unite local people in defense of their land and way of life, local resistance movements have often been driven by a mix of patriotic feeling, tribal bonds, and complaints against foreign incursions.

Afghanistan's capacity to defy outside pressure and preserve some degree of autonomy has been greatly aided by the interaction between tribalism, guerrilla warfare, and local resistance. These elements have given Afghans the opportunity to profit from their familiarity with the region, take advantage of the deficiencies of the occupying troops, and mobilize local populations to fight foreign occupation. Afghanistan has a reputation as a difficult and unconquerable region due to its long history of tribal allegiance and the tenacity of guerilla warfare.

It is crucial to remember that tribalism may lead to internal disputes and splits even while it can be a source of strength and resistance. Tribal rivalries and power conflicts have sometimes impeded attempts to maintain national stability and unity. Guerrilla warfare and local resistance have also led to protracted battles and cycles of bloodshed inside the nation, notwithstanding their effectiveness in fending off invaders.

Understanding the intricacies of Afghanistan's history, wars, and current difficulties requires an understanding of the role of tribes, guerrilla warfare, and local resistance. It illustrates the Afghan people's tenacity and resolve in defending their territory and sovereignty as well as the complex sociopolitical processes that continue to determine the course of the nation.

14.3 The impact of foreign interventions on Afghanistan's resilience

The adaptability of Afghanistan and its people has been significantly impacted by foreign operations. Afghanistan has historically been a site of conflict between opposing empires and a target for other forces attempting to rule the area. Afghanistan's social structure, political stability, and economic growth have been influenced by these interventions, which are often marked by military invasions, political meddling, and efforts to impose foreign ideologies.

Foreign interventions have helped the Afghan people develop a spirit of resiliency. A communal sense of resistance and tenacity has been fostered by the nation's lengthy history of fending against foreign invaders. Afghans have often shown that they can adapt, organize, and resist invading armies. The Afghan people's tenacity, which is built in a strong sense of loyalty to their country, culture, and traditions, has been a major factor in their ability to endure outside influences and preserve their unique national identity.

Tribal and communal ties have often been reinforced as a result of foreign operations in reaction to external threats. In the past, Afghans have united to protect their country against foreign domination, despite differences in tribe and ethnicity. The feeling of camaraderie across many groups has been strengthened by these common experiences of struggle and pain. The resilience of Afghanistan is largely attributed to its people's capacity to come together in the face of external difficulties by taking courage from their common history and collective identity.

Foreign operations have made it more important than ever for Afghanistan's rich cultural legacy to be preserved. Foreign powers have often encountered opposition in their efforts to impose their own ideas and values, which has increased cultural pride and preservation. Afghan culture has fought valiantly to preserve its cultural customs, dialects, and religious beliefs because they see them as crucial parts of their identity. Afghan culture has persevered in the face of external pressure, which has helped the nation keep its own cultural character.

Foreign operations have significantly complicated and disrupted Afghanistan's stability, despite its resiliency. Numerous people have been displaced, killed, and experienced social unrest as a consequence of wars, political unrest, and the invasion of foreign troops. The nation has gone through times of instability, internal strife, and divides stoked by outside influence. Afghanistan's resiliency has been put to the test by these difficulties, which have also slowed down its advancement in governance, infrastructure building, and socioeconomic development.

Foreign military operations have had a long-lasting effect on Afghanistan's political, social, and economic structures. Foreign occupations, proxy warfare, and intervention in domestic affairs have left behind complicated dynamics and continuing conflicts in the nation. The power dynamics in the area have also changed as a result of these operations, with surrounding nations often competing for influence and using Afghanistan as a battlefield for their own objectives. The long-term repercussions of foreign operations continue to influence Afghanistan's toughness and capacity to overcome obstacles.

Foreign interventions have a complicated and multidimensional effect on Afghanistan's capacity for resilience. Although these actions have created considerable difficulties and interruptions, they have also strengthened the Afghan people's spirit of resistance, cohesion, and cultural preservation. Afghans' steadfast perseverance and dedication to preserving their country are shown by the country's capacity to defy outside pressure and retain its distinctive character.

Chapter 15

Lessons from Afghanistan's Resilience

15.1 Analyzing the resilience of Afghanistan against superpowers

Afghanistan's history is distinguished by its incredible tenacity in the face of superpowers throughout the years. The nation has often shown that it is capable of fending off the military strength and political sway of superpowers like the Soviet Union and the United States. Afghanistan has remained resilient in the face of these superpowers due to a number of factors:

- Geographical Difficulties: For foreign conquerors, Afghanistan's rough and rocky topography has presented substantial difficulties. Large military troops have traditionally found it difficult to efficiently manage and govern the area due to the hard landscape, which includes huge deserts, deep valleys, and high mountain ranges like the Hindu Kush. The topography of Afghanistan has naturally favored guerrilla warfare, enabling local resistance fighters to use hit-and-run tactics and capitalize on their familiarity with the terrain.

- Population that is Determined and Resilient: The Afghan people have shown incredible resiliency in the face of hardship. The ardent defense of their independence, cultural identity, and way of life dates back many years. Afghans' capacity to withstand and fight foreign rule has been greatly aided by their feeling of pride and solidarity. Their resiliency in the face of superpowers has been fueled by their deep devotion to their land and readiness to make sacrifices for it.

- Tribal Organizations and Local Resistance: Afghanistan's tribal organizations have organized local resistance against foreign invaders in a substantial way. Tribal networks and allegiances have played a crucial role in organizing local warriors and supporting resistance groups. Tribal systems are decentralized, making it difficult for outside forces to impose their will throughout the whole nation. Local resistance groups, often based on tribal ties, have shown tenacity in the face of foreign incursions by using guerilla warfare strategies and capitalizing on their local terrain expertise.

- Historical Context and Lessons Learned: Invaders such as the British Empire, the Soviet Union, and the United States have all been repelled by Afghanistan in the past. Each incident of resistance has offered insightful lessons to succeeding generations. The collective memory of prior conflicts has influenced the Afghan people's tenacity and commitment to maintain their sovereignty. They have a strong sense of self-confidence in their capacity to defeat outside forces thanks to their experience fighting off prior superpowers.

Afghanistan has gained support and solidarity from a number of nations and international players that are sympathetic to its cause. This help has included anything from military assistance and training to diplomatic support and humanitarian supplies. Afghanistan's resilience has been strengthened by international support, which has given it resources, knowledge, and a feeling of community in the face of outside challenges.

While Afghanistan's ability to hold its own against superpowers is impressive, it is also crucial to recognize the immense suffering, displaced populations, and damage brought on by these battles. The Afghan people's steadfast perseverance has come at a high price; the nation has endured protracted periods of violence, instability, and tragedy. To promote long-term peace, prosperity, and resilience for Afghanistan's citizens, a comprehensive and inclusive strategy is necessary given the country's persistent difficulties and complexity.

15.2 Examining the limitations and challenges faced by the invaders

The constraints and problems encountered during the Soviet and American invasions of Afghanistan demonstrate the complexity and difficulty of doing business in the area. These restrictions have helped to make the Afghan resistance more tenacious and resilient:

- Support from Regional friends: Thanks to Afghanistan's position and closeness to other nations, the Afghan resistance has been able to find sympathetic regional friends. Supportive neighbors have helped Afghan fighters by offering safe havens, access to supplies, and other resources, making it more difficult for foreign armies to fully take control of the country.

- Cost and Public Attitude: Long-term military operations in Afghanistan have been very expensive in terms of money, people, and public sentiment. Domestic support for ongoing military operations has been weakened by the length of these wars, as well as their cost in lives and money. The difficulties encountered by foreign powers have increased because to the local and global reaction against the financial and human costs of the invasions.

- Guerilla warfare and asymmetrical tactics: In the past, Afghan resistance fighters have used hit-and-run assaults, ambushes, and blending in with the local populace as guerilla warfare techniques. These asymmetric strategies have shown to be successful in thwarting conventional forces and taking advantage of the weaknesses of the invaders. It has been difficult for foreign troops to properly identify and combat Afghan militants due to their ability to operate in tiny, dispersed formations and their familiarity with the rough terrain.

- Geographical and Weather Challenges: Foreign invaders have faced considerable logistical difficulties due to Afghanistan's hard and varied topography, which includes mountains, deserts, and severe weather. The challenging terrain makes it difficult for soldiers and equipment to travel, leaving supply lines open to assault. Cold winters and high heat have made military operations much more difficult, limiting the mobility and endurance of occupying soldiers.

- Political Landscape: Regional power struggles and fragmentation characterize Afghanistan's political environment. Rival groups, tribal conflicts, and racial tensions have been recurring themes throughout the nation's history. The goal of constructing a stable and cohesive Afghan administration that supports the interests of foreign powers has been made more difficult by these internal conflicts. Long-term stability initiatives have been hampered by the absence of a unified political body and conflicting power centers.

Foreign soldiers operating in Afghanistan have encountered major cultural and linguistic obstacles. Afghan society is distinguished by its varied ethnic and tribal make-up as well as a well established sense of cultural and religious identity. Foreign soldiers have found it difficult to comprehend and navigate this complicated socio-cultural environment, which has hampered their capacity to develop effective relationships with local populations and gain their confidence in order to collect information.

Historical Background and Invasions' Past Lessons The history of unsuccessful invasions in Afghanistan, particularly those by the British and Soviet Union, has taught future attackers important lessons. The Afghan people are motivated to persist in the face of future invasions by their collective memory of effective resistance against foreign domination. The perseverance of the Afghan people has been influenced by their country's turbulent past, which has inspired them to oppose and protect it.

The perseverance and tenacity of the Afghan resistance against foreign invaders has been aided by these constraints and difficulties as a whole. They draw attention to the difficulties of functioning in Afghanistan's particular setting, where historical, cultural, and geopolitical variables are important. Any foreign force wishing to participate in the area successfully must comprehend and meet these obstacles.

15.3 Lessons for future military interventions and counter-insurgency operations

The military incursions and counter-insurgency operations in Afghanistan have taught us numerous valuable lessons that will help us in our future work. To increase the efficiency and reduce the difficulties experienced by foreign troops, it is essential to comprehend the following lessons:

- Comprehensive Approach: Military interventions must adopt a comprehensive strategy that takes into account political, economic, and social factors in addition to military actions. It is unlikely to maintain lasting stability by relying exclusively on military power without addressing the underlying political resentments, economic inequalities, and social divides. A complete strategy should include development projects, governance changes, and assistance for regional institutions.

- Building Relationships and Trust: Effective community connections and trust-building are essential for success. This calls for consultation with regional authorities, tribe elders, and powerful individuals, as well as participation of the general populace in decision-making. Gaining information, combating insurgent propaganda, and securing support for detecting and removing dangers all depend on building confidence and credibility with the local populace.

- Building Local Capacity and Ownership: Instead of merely depending on foreign troops, there should be an emphasis on strengthening local security forces and institutions. Providing local forces with training and equipment enables them to play a bigger part in guaranteeing security and stability. Sustainable results depend on encouraging local ownership and giving local communities the tools they need to manage their own security.

- Flexibility and Adaptability: Military operations need to be able to adjust quickly to changing conditions on the ground. Insurgents often change their tactics and plans, requiring the occupying troops to react quickly. To successfully combat insurgency and react to new threats, flexibility in the employment of military assets, information collection, and decision-making procedures is crucial.

- Restraint and Military Force in Balance: The use of military force must be proportionate and restrained. Overuse of force or collateral damage may breed discontent, encourage the recruitment of insurgents, and jeopardize the authority of the occupying troops. Gaining the favor of the local populace requires placing a strong emphasis on the preservation of civilian life, observing cultural sensitivities, and minimizing civilian losses.

- Coordination and cooperation: It is crucial for all parties involved, including international players, regional powers, and local partners, to work effectively together. Military interventions may be more successful if there is a coherent strategy and a common knowledge of the goals and tactics. Additionally, coordination promotes resource efficiency, addresses regional dynamics, and prevents effort duplication.

Military interventions and counter-insurgency operations need both a long-term commitment as well as patience. It takes years to establish stability and enduring peace; fast solutions or hasty retreats might trigger a return of insurrection. In order to secure the consolidation of benefits and avoid a security vacuum, ongoing assistance and participation are required.

Understanding the local environment is crucial for any military action since it informs decisions about social dynamics, cultural practices, and historical backdrop. Building connections, winning over the community, and successfully battling an insurgency all depend on having a solid awareness of the political, social, and ethnic milieu. Apathy, misconceptions, and unexpected consequences might result from failing to grasp or misinterpreting the local context.

Reflecting on the triumphs and failures of earlier military operations is essential for learning from past mistakes. Understanding the lessons learned from Afghanistan and other situations that are comparable may aid in future decision-making, prevent errors from being made again, and increase the efficiency of military interventions and counter-insurgency operations.

Future military operations and counter-insurgency operations may be better prepared to handle the complex problems presented by such situations, improve their chances of success, and reduce the dangers and unintended effects connected with international operations by using these lessons.

Chapter 16

The Impact of Hari Singh Nalwa's Victories

16.1 Influence on regional power dynamics

The regional power dynamics under Nalwa's reign were significantly influenced by his military prowess and leadership. His effective operations and the strengthening of Sikh rule in the Sikh Empire's northwest border area changed the balance of power and completely transformed the region's political environment. The following are some crucial elements of Nalwa's impact on the dynamics of regional power:

- Sikh Empire Expansion: Under Nalwa's direction, the Sikh Empire grew to include parts of what is now Pakistan, including Peshawar, Multan, and Kashmir. The Sikh Empire's influence and strength expanded as a result of its expansion, making it a significant regional force in South Asia.

- Afghan-Sikh Rivalry: Nalwa's wins against Afghan soldiers put Afghan authorities in the northwest border area under pressure. Afghan lands and their ability to maintain control over the area were directly threatened by the Sikh Empire's geographical expansion and military might. The conflict between the Sikhs and the Afghans altered the balance of power in the area and heightened the struggle for influence.

- Balance of Power: The Sikh Empire's geographical dominance and Nalwa's military victories in the area helped create a new system of power relations. Invading other regional powers like the Afghans and different indigenous Pashtun tribes, the Sikhs rose to become a powerful force. The Sikh Empire became a more major factor in the northwest border area as a result of its territorial growth and military might.

- Sikh Control and Influence: Nalwa's administration as governor of Peshawar furthered Sikh control in the area. He carried out administrative changes, built up the nation's infrastructure, and promoted commerce, all of which increased Sikh rule and authority over the regions. As surrounding nations had to manage the expanding influence and geographical reach of the Sikh Empire, this influence had an impact on the dynamics of regional power.

- Legacy of Sikh Rule: The Sikh Empire's impact and Nalwa's leadership have left a permanent mark on the balance of power in the area. The effect of Sikh rule and their military might continued to affect how people saw power and influence in the northwest border area long after the Sikh Empire had fallen. The political ambitions and affiliations of many local powers were impacted by the legacy of Nalwa's triumphs and the Sikh Empire's rule over important provinces.

- Influence on Subsequent Conflicts: Nalwa's military successes and techniques were studied by succeeding military commanders and included into the historical narrative. Future military operations in the area were influenced by his creative strategies for conflict resolution and his aptitude at navigating complicated tribal dynamics. Beyond his lifetime, Nalwa's legacy and influence on regional power dynamics were still significant.

Tribal dynamics in the area were influenced by Nalwa's relationships with other Pashtun clans and regional groups. His diplomatic efforts, military victories, and political philosophies had an impact on how various tribal groups interacted with one another and with the Sikh Empire. The shifting regional environment was influenced by the realignment of tribal allegiances and the creation of new power dynamics.

In conclusion, Sardar Hari Singh Nalwa had a considerable impact on the regional power dynamics of his period via his military achievements, the growth of the Sikh Empire, and his leadership of the northwest border area. The Sikh Empire's emergence as a significant regional force, its competition with the Afghans, and the realignment of tribal dynamics had a long-lasting effect on the region's political environment. Even after the fall of the Sikh

Empire, Nalwa's legacy and impact remained to affect regional power relations.

16.2 Effects on the Sikh Empire's expansion and stability

During his lifetime, Sardar Hari Singh Nalwa was very important to the development and continuity of the Sikh Empire. His military prowess, leadership abilities, and administrative changes had a big impact on the expansion and stability of the empire. The following are some of the main results of Nalwa's contributions:

- Territorial Expansion: Nalwa's military operations significantly contributed to the Sikh Empire's territorial growth. He oversaw prosperous excursions into places like Peshawar, Kashmir, and Multan, greatly expanding the empire's realm. In addition to expanding the empire's political power and authority over key areas, Nalwa's successes also increased its geographical bounds.
- Consolidation of Power: Nalwa's strategic leadership and vision were crucial in securing the Sikh Empire's hold on recently conquered lands. He introduced administrative reforms, set up efficient governance structures, and made sure the occupied territories were properly run. He played a role in the general consolidation of power within the empire by preserving stability and establishing Sikh authority in these areas.
- Security and Defense: Nalwa strengthened the frontiers of the empire and adopted creative

defense tactics while leading the Sikh army. To safeguard the empire's borders and prevent prospective invasions, he built several forts and defensive fortifications. These defenses not only guaranteed the safety of the empire but also served as representations of Sikh might and intimidation.

- Economic Prosperity: Nalwa's focus on building infrastructure and promoting commerce had a good effect on the empire's economy. He launched a number of construction initiatives, including as the building of marketplaces, roads, and canals, which boosted economic development and enabled commerce throughout the empire. The Sikh Empire was more stable and prosperous overall because to the increasing commerce and economic activities.

- Cultural Integration: Nalwa understood the value of integrating cultures and promoting peaceable living within the empire. Despite ruling over Sikh-controlled areas, he recognized and upheld the cultural and religious traditions of other people there. The stability of the empire and the allegiance of its varied people were aided by this inclusive attitude, which promoted a feeling of unity and social cohesiveness.

- Strength and Deterrence in the Military: Nalwa's military victories and the general might of the Sikh army under his leadership acted as a deterrence against possible foes. Nalwa's strategic prowess together with the reputation of the Sikh warriors served as a deterrence and prevented other armies from challenging the empire's dominance. The Sikh Empire's stability and deterrence were aided by its military might.

- Impact & Inspiration: Nalwa's services to the Sikh Empire inspired later generations and created a long-lasting impact. His leadership abilities, organizational innovations, and military prowess became the gold standard for Sikh commanders and leaders in the future. The leaders of the empire were inspired and motivated by Nalwa's legacy to maintain and advance the growth and stability he had achieved.

Sardar Singh Hari The growth and continuity of the Sikh Empire were significantly impacted by Nalwa's efforts. The expansion, unification, and stability of the empire were significantly shaped by his military victories, administrative reforms, and focus on defense, economic prosperity, cultural integration, and military might. The empire's power and durability were enhanced by the subsequent generations who were inspired by Nalwa's legacy.

16.3 Nalwa's significance in Indian and Afghan history

Sardar Hari Singh Nalwa's military prowess, leadership skills, and contributions to the region's political environment give him a special place in both Indian and Afghan history. The following main points underline Nalwa's importance in Indian and Afghan history:

- Defender of the Sikh Empire: Nalwa played a significant part in the history of the Sikh Empire as both the governor of Peshawar and a well-known Sikh commander. His military prowess and strategic insight were important in the expansion and consolidation of the empire's realms. Nalwa's accomplishments in protecting the Sikh Empire from outside attacks increased his position as a hero in Sikh history.

- Symbol of Sikh Valor and Unity: Nalwa's military prowess and leadership have elevated him to the status of a Sikh national hero. He served as an example of the Sikhs' martial traditions and came to symbolize their bravery, tenacity, and commitment to defending their religion and sovereignty. Sikhs are still motivated by Nalwa's legacy as a testament to fortitude and Sikh identity.

- Influence on Indian Military Traditions: Indian military traditions were significantly influenced by Nalwa's creative warfare ideas and tactics. Military historians and strategists continue to research and respect his methods of fortification, defense, and guerilla warfare. The contributions of Nalwa have shaped military thought in the area and have had an impact on later generations of Indian military officers.

- Role in Afghan History: The Battle of Jamrud and Nalwa's campaigns, in particular, have had a great impact on Afghan history. Nalwa's relations with

Afghanistan and the Afghan kings have also had a significant impact on Afghan history. His wins against Afghan troops put the Afghan hegemony in the northwest border region to the test and altered the regional power relations. In Afghan history records, Nalwa is regarded as a powerful foe and a symbol of resistance.

- Afghan Folklore and Legends: Afghan mythology and tales have been influenced by Nalwa's adventures, which has increased his historical relevance in Afghanistan. His military successes and the stories surrounding his courage and fighting prowess are still told in the region's folklore. In the collective memory of the Afghan people, Nalwa's character has transcended national and cultural barriers to become a picture of bravery and valor.

- Cross-Cultural Links: Nalwa's encounters with other groups, such as Afghans, Sikhs, and Pashtuns, show off his contribution to promoting cross-cultural links. With the numerous Afghan leaders and tribes he maintained diplomatic ties with, he won their respect and esteem. Nalwa's importance as a bridge-builder between many populations in the area was influenced by his ability to maneuver multiple cultural and religious environments.

- Historical Considerations on Power Dynamics: Nalwa's military prowess and his participation in the power conflicts of his day have had a long-

> lasting influence on our comprehension of regional power dynamics. His battles and triumphs shed insight on the intricate relationships that existed between the Sikh Empire, Afghanistan, and local Pashtun tribes, among other regional forces. The relevance of Nalwa comes from his status as a historical figure who influenced the regional political and military scene.

In both Indian and Afghan history, Nalwa has had a significant impact on both countries. He stands for Sikh bravery and togetherness as a well-known Sikh commander and protector of the Sikh Empire. His combat tactics have affected Indian military customs, while the stories and mythology of Afghanistan have been inspired by his part in Afghan history. Nalwa's historical importance in both Indian and Afghan history is further enhanced by his influence on power dynamics in the area and his cross-cultural relationships.

Chapter 17

Nalwa's Personality and Leadership Style

17.1 Understanding Nalwa's character and values

Nalwa's morals and character had a significant role in the development of his illustrious military career and achievements to the Sikh Empire. Nalwa's character and ideals are highlighted by the following significant factors:

- Courage and Fearlessness: Nalwa was the epitome of unrelenting tenacity and fearlessness on the battlefield. He courageously led his forces into combat, often leading the charge, displaying his own bravery and motivating his troops. Nalwa's lack of fear gave him the courage to take on powerful foes and navigate difficult circumstances with tenacity and resolution.

- Commitment and dedication: Nalwa had an unflinching commitment and dedication to the Sikh Empire and its principles. He showed unwavering commitment to his Sikh comrades and the values they upheld by dedicating his life to serving the empire and its citizens. Nalwa's zeal to the Sikh cause served as the impetus for both his military prowess and his unrelenting commitment to the security and growth of the empire.

- Leadership and Strategic Vision: Nalwa had great leadership and strategic vision. He was able to understand intricate military circumstances, come up with winning plans, and carry them out precisely. Beyond the battlefield, Nalwa demonstrated effective leadership by governing the areas under his authority and enacting administrative changes to promote peace and prosperity.

- Regard for Diversity and Inclusion: Nalwa's regard for diversity and inclusion was a defining quality of his personality. He accepted the religious and cultural customs of other populations inside the Sikh-controlled areas while being a Sikh leader. The inclusive style of Nalwa contributed to the peace and tranquility of the empire by fostering a feeling of oneness among many ethnic groups.

- Justice and Fairness: Nalwa has a reputation for being devoted to justice and fairness. Regardless of their origins or social standing, he made sure that his warriors and people received justice and respect. Nalwa's focus on justice and fairness won him the esteem and respect of people he ruled over and contributed to the general stability and prosperity of the lands he governed.

- Discipline and Perseverance: Nalwa maintained strong discipline among his soldiers and shown unshakable determination in the face of difficulty. His men exhibited a sense of professionalism and discipline that improved their performance on the battlefield. Nalwa's willpower helped him overcome many obstacles and defeats, enhancing his standing as a fearsome leader.

- Humility and Humane Treatment: Despite his military accomplishments and his prominent position, Nalwa retained his modesty and treated people with respect and compassion. He was renowned for treating prisoners of war with kindness and making an attempt to reduce the number of civilian losses in battle. Both his warriors and his enemies respected Nalwa for his humanitarian attitude.

Characteristics and principles of Nalwa were loyalty, bravery, inclusiveness, justice, discipline, persistence, humility, and compassionate treatment. These characteristics had a crucial role in his military successes and the administration of the areas he controlled. In both Sikh and more general historical settings, Nalwa's character and principles have inspired people and served as a monument to the virtues of leadership and service.

17.2 Leadership qualities that contributed to his success

In order to achieve such extraordinary success as a military commander and administrator, Sardar Hari Singh Nalwa had a number of essential leadership traits. He was able to command the Sikh army, grow the Sikh Empire, and rule the areas he controlled thanks in large part to these characteristics. The following are a few of the traits of a successful leader that Nalwa possessed:

- Strategic Vision: Nalwa had a great strategic vision that enabled him to evaluate challenging military circumstances and create workable solutions. He had a thorough awareness of the geopolitical dynamics of the area and was able to predict his enemies' intentions and course of action. Nalwa's ability to see the big picture let him make wise choices and modify his plans as needed, which helped him succeed on the battlefield.

- Fearless Bravery: Nalwa had remarkable levels of both bravery and fearlessness. He commanded his men from the front, giving them courage and motivating them to take on difficult tasks. In the midst of difficulty, Nalwa's bravery enabled him to make brave choices and take calculated risks, displaying his everlasting dedication to the Sikh cause.

- Brilliant Tactical Decisions: One of Nalwa's leadership traits was brilliant tactical decision-making. He was skilled at deploying his men to get a tactical advantage and had a thorough command of military tactics. Nalwa's tactical prowess allowed him to outmaneuver and outwit his adversaries, often winning against forces who were numerically superior.

- Strong Leadership Presence: Nalwa had a strong leadership aura and had a commanding presence. His magnetic personality and charm attracted warriors who were devoted to him. Nalwa set the bar high by setting an example of discipline, professionalism, and commitment to his work. His leadership style encouraged his soldiers to feel a sense of purpose and camaraderie, which increased their efficacy on the battlefield.

- Sound Decision-Making: Nalwa's success depended on his capacity to make judgments that were both sound and timely. He had outstanding judgment and analytical abilities that allowed him to weigh the benefits and drawbacks of various actions. Nalwa's ability to make decisions enabled him to take advantage of chances, deal with obstacles in a wise way, and keep the initiative in combat.

- Skills in Administration and Organization: Nalwa excelled in administration and organization, especially in his position as governor of Peshawar. He encouraged infrastructural and economic development initiatives, built administrative institutions, and put into place efficient governance mechanisms. Nalwa's administrative and organizational skills made the areas under his rule stable and prosperous.

- Tenacity and Resilience: Nalwa's success was largely due to his tenacity and resilience. Throughout his military career, he encountered many obstacles, disappointments, and personal losses, yet he never wavered in his dedication to the Sikh cause. Nalwa's fortitude enabled him to recover from setbacks, learn from his errors, and keep pursuing success.

- Ethics and Moral Leadership: Nalwa exercised moral leadership by abiding by a strict code of ethics. He showed justice, respect, and decency to both his army and people. The devotion and adoration of people under Nalwa's direction was a result of his moral and ethical leadership, which helped to foster a feeling of cohesion and common purpose.

Nalwa combined strategic vision, courage, tactical acumen, commanding leadership presence, wise judgment, administrative and organizational abilities, fortitude, and moral leadership. Together, these traits helped him succeed as a military leader and governor. The leadership legacy of Nalwa is still an inspiration and a role model for leaders in both military and non-military settings.

17.3 Nalwa's enduring reputation as a warrior

Sardar Hari Singh Nalwa's legendary status as a warrior endures today due to his outstanding military accomplishments and the lasting impression he had on history. Nalwa had extraordinary courage, keen strategic judgment, and unflinching devotion to the Sikh Empire throughout his career. His reputation as a fighter is based on a number of important elements:

- Triumphs against Powerful Opponents: Nalwa's reputation as a warrior was based on his many triumphs over powerful opponents. He commanded Sikh soldiers in fights against Afghan and other regional powers effectively, often outlasting stronger, more well-equipped armies. His military acumen and reputation as a fierce fighter were cemented by his ability to outmaneuver, outsmart, and beat his adversaries in combat.

- Military Leadership and Command: Nalwa's reputation as a warrior was greatly influenced by his leadership and command abilities. His warriors were devoted to him and respected him; they looked up to him for his leadership qualities and steadfast commitment to their goal. In addition to helping his warriors succeed, Nalwa's capacity for inspiring and motivating them on the battlefield furthered his standing as a feared warrior.

- Military Success Legacy: Nalwa's military triumphs have left a lasting impression, which has aided in maintaining his standing as a fierce warrior. His achievements not only increased the size of the Sikh Empire but also guaranteed its security. Nalwa's military actions helped the Sikhs take control of the area and left a lasting impact that is still felt today.

- Folklore and Tales: Nalwa's adventures and successes have been incorporated into folklore and tales throughout time. Generation after

> generation has handed down tales of his bravery, strategic genius, and unbreakable spirit, further solidifying his status as a renowned warrior. These stories have remained captivating and inspiring, solidifying Nalwa's status as one of history's most valiant soldiers.

The fact that Sardar Hari Singh Nalwa has maintained his reputation as a warrior throughout time is a testimonial to his extraordinary military prowess, unflinching courage, and leadership qualities. His legacy, which serves as a reminder of his important contributions to the Sikh Empire and his position in the annals of military history, continues to arouse admiration and respect.

Chapter 18

Cultural and Social Impact of Nalwa's Victories

18.1 Nalwa's influence on Sikh identity and pride

The impact of Nalwa on Sikh pride and identity is significant and lasting. He became a legendary character in Sikh history as a result of his outstanding military accomplishments, persistent devotion to the Sikh Empire, and embodiment of Sikh principles. The following are some significant facets of Nalwa's impact on Sikh identity and pride:

- Defending Sikh Sovereignty: The Sikh community was greatly moved by Nalwa's unshakable dedication to upholding the sovereignty of the Sikh Empire. His successes against foreign foes demonstrated the Sikhs' fortitude and power, fostering a feeling of pride and identity among Sikhs as a fighting people capable of defending their own interests.

- Promoting Sikh Ideals: Nalwa set a great example for the Sikh community by upholding the Sikh ideals of bravery, fairness, and selflessness. Sikh ideals served as the foundation for his leadership on the battlefield and in the administration of the areas under his authority, urging Sikhs to adopt and defend these beliefs in their own life.

- Expansion of the Sikh Empire: Increased feeling of Sikh identity and pride was brought on by Nalwa's role in expanding the Sikh Empire and cementing Sikh authority. His military efforts established Sikh dominance in areas that had previously been ruled by other nations, strengthening Sikh sovereignty and fostering a feeling of Sikh identity and pride in the areas under Sikh administration.

- Symbol of Sikh Martial Heritage: Nalwa has endured as a symbol of Sikh martial heritage due to his courage and military competence. His military prowess embodies the spirit of Sikh warriors, inspiring the Sikh community to uphold justice and righteousness and honor their great martial tradition.

- Inspiration for Future Generations: Sikhs in the future might draw inspiration from Nalwa's legacy. Sikhs are motivated to embrace their history, maintain Sikh ideals, and make constructive contributions to their communities and society at large by his leadership, courage, and steadfast devotion to the Sikh cause. A feeling of Sikh identity and pride that spans generations is fostered through Nalwa's impact.

- Cultural and Historical Significance: Nalwa's contributions to Sikh history and culture have increased his standing as a renowned person within the Sikh community. His accomplishments are honored throughout Sikh literature, art, and oral traditions, which guarantees that his legacy will go on as a crucial component of Sikh identity and pride.

The impact of Nalwa on Sikh pride and identity is extensive. His unflinching dedication to Sikh principles, his military prowess, and his personification of Sikh combat customs have made a lasting impression on Sikh history. The Sikh community continues to feel pride and identification in Nalwa because it represents Sikh bravery, tenacity, and sovereignty.

18.2 Impact on Punjabi literature, art, and folklore

The influence of Nalwa on Punjabi literature, art, and culture is substantial. His outstanding leadership abilities, adherence to Sikh principles, and military prowess have impacted and inspired several kinds of artistic expression in the Punjabi cultural landscape. Here are a few ways Nalwa's legacy continues to have an impact:

- Folklore and Oral Tradition: Punjabi folklore and oral tradition have included Nalwa's adventures and valiant actions to a great extent. His memory is preserved by the stories that have been handed down through the years about his courage, strategic brilliance, and undying dedication to the Sikh cause. These tales serve to inspire and promote pride in Punjabi culture in addition to providing entertainment.

- Literary Works: Punjabi literature has preserved Nalwa's life and accomplishments. His military battles and leadership have been praised by poets, authors, and historians in their creative creations. His bravery and achievements to the Sikh Empire are often portrayed in epic poetry, historical fiction, and biographies, preserving his legacy for future generations.

- Artistic Representations: In Punjabi art, Nalwa has been shown in many ways. His courage and leadership are often shown in war situations in paintings, sculptures, and other visual arts. In addition to accurately capturing Nalwa's physical attributes, these creative representations also reflect the essence of Sikh martial culture and arouse awe and devotion.

- Cultural Festivals and Celebrations: In Punjab, a number of cultural festivals and activities are held to remember and honor Nalwa. The occasion of Nalwa Diwas, which commemorates the anniversary of his birth, is a time when people get together to honor and celebrate his accomplishments. These gatherings provide a venue for showcasing Punjabi artwork, music, and dance, further enhancing the Nalwa region's cultural legacy.

- Source of Inspiration for Painters and Authors: Nalwa's narrative is a source of great inspiration for authors, painters, and filmmakers. His valor, bravery, and military prowess provide as a great narrative setting for literary works. Numerous Punjabi authors and artists are inspired by Nalwa's life to produce gripping poetry, books, and films that perfectly reflect his spirit and the historical setting in which he lived.

- Symbol of Punjabi Pride: Nalwa has come to represent the identity and pride of the Punjabi people. His achievements in the military, leadership skills, and adherence to Sikh principles serve as a symbol of the fortitude, resiliency, and cultural legacy of the Punjabi people. The tradition of Nalwa strengthens Punjabis' feeling of pride and encourages a closer ties to their historical and cultural origins.

Punjabi literature, art, and folklore have all been greatly influenced by Nalwa. The Punjabi community has been motivated to engage in storytelling, creative expression, cultural festivities, and a feeling of pride by his larger-than-life presence, military prowess, and embodiment of Sikh principles. Nalwa's influence is still felt today in a variety of artistic mediums, guaranteeing that his contributions to Punjabi history and culture will be loved and honored for many years to come.

18.3 Commemorative traditions and celebrations

Celebrations and commemorative customs are essential to commemorating Sardar Hari Singh Nalwa's heritage and preserving his memory. These customs are ways of recognizing his contributions to Sikh history and culture and of showing thanks, admiration, and respect. The following are some of the commemoration customs and events related to Nalwa:

- Nalwa Diwas: On the anniversary of his birth, there is an annual festival called Nalwa Diwas, often referred to as Nalwa Day. Everywhere in the globe, Sikhs and Punjabis celebrate it with tremendous fervor. Activities that honor Nalwa's life, accomplishments, and the principles he upheld include religious processions, community meetings, lectures, exhibits, and cultural performances.

- Gurudwara Programs: Numerous Gurudwaras (Sikh houses of worship) host special activities and programs to pay tribute to Sardar Hari Singh Nalwa. Religious services, kirtan (devotional song), and speeches centered on Nalwa's life, his contributions to the Sikh Empire, and his adherence to Sikh values are some of the events that make up this schedule. The Sikh community comes together to honor him and draw inspiration from his heroic life.

- Historical Exhibitions: Exhibitions honoring Sardar Hari Singh Nalwa are often organized by museums, historical societies, and cultural institutions. Visitors to these displays gain knowledge about Nalwa's life, his military exploits, and the historical setting in which he lived through seeing relics, manuscripts, paintings, and other historical things connected to him. People may learn about his accomplishments via immersive displays of this kind.

- Folk Performances: Folk dances, music, and theater are often used to commemorate Nalwa's legacy. Nalwa's bravery and heroism are depicted in traditional art forms by folk artists and troupes. These performances seek to not only amuse the audience but also to convey his tales and instill a feeling of pride in them.

- Literary and Cultural Events: Sardar Hari Singh Nalwa is often discussed, spoken on, and presented at literary festivals, cultural events, and seminars devoted to Sikh history and culture. To discuss their findings, research, and opinions on Nalwa's life and legacy, academics, historians, and authors assemble. These occasions foster a greater appreciation of his work and provide a forum for intellectual discussion.

- Artistic Expressions: Sardar Hari Singh Nalwa serves as an inspiration for sculptors, painters, and other creatives. Paintings, sculptures, and other works of art honor his military strength and leadership characteristics while capturing his famous and heroic demeanor. These works of art help to remember Nalwa's life and accomplishments by acting as a visual reflection of his legacy.

The commemorative customs and events held in honor of Sardar Hari Singh Nalwa are evidence of his contributions' ongoing influence. These occasions and activities provide chances for people and communities to reflect on, commemorate, and celebrate his life, motivating future generations to uphold the ideals he embodied and to be proud of their Sikh heritage. These customs guarantee that Nalwa's legacy lives on to inspire and educate future generations about his vital contribution to Sikh history by upholding his memory.

Chapter 19

The Life of Nalwa Beyond Warfare

19.1 Nalwa's personal life and relationships

Sardar Hari Singh Nalwa had a personal life that influenced his whole character and ideals, despite the fact that he is well known for his military prowess and leadership. Aspects of Nalwa's private life and relationships include the following:

- Family and Upbringing: In Gujranwala, Punjab, in 1791, Nalwa was born into a Sikh household. Gurdial Singh, his father, was well-known in the Sikh community. Nalwa was raised in a setting that was strongly influenced by Sikh traditions, which had a big impact on how he identified and valued things.

- Marriage and Children: Nalwa wed Sada Kaur, a Kanhaiya Misl member and the daughter of Sardar Gurdit Singh. Fateh Singh and Jawahar Singh were their two sons. As he dealt with the difficulties of his military career, Nalwa's marriage and family life gave him a feeling of support and security.

- Relationships with Maharaja Ranjit Singh: Maharaja Ranjit Singh, the Sikh Empire's founder, and Nalwa were close friends. Nalwa's appointment as governor of Peshawar, which demonstrated the Maharaja's faith and confidence in him, was a result of his military skill. Their cooperation and mutual regard were important to the growth and stability of the Sikh Empire.

- Camaraderie with fellow Sikh leaders: Solid friendships with other major Sikh leaders of the day, such as Diwan Mulraj, Akali Phoola Singh, and Sher Singh Attariwala, were shared by Nalwa. They collaborated to protect and expand Sikh lands because they had a same goal for the Sikh Empire. The Sikh leadership benefited from a feeling of togetherness and camaraderie as a result of these connections.

- Respect for Sikh Principles: Sikh beliefs and principles have a significant impact on Nalwa's relationships and personal life. He was an excellent example of the Sikh idea of "Sarbat da Bhala" (welfare of everyone) via his equitable and fair rule, kindness to his warriors and people, and commitment to preserving Sikh sovereignty. Nalwa's behavior demonstrated his dedication to following Sikh principles.

- Devotion to Sikhism: Nalwa's personal life was characterized by a strong dedication to the Sikhism. He was renowned for his devotion to Sikh ceremonies, daily practice of saying prayers, and reverence for the Guru Granth Sahib, the Sikh holy book. His spirituality and sense of religion gave him inner strength and direction all through his life.

Understanding Nalwa's personal life and relationships might help us better comprehend the ideals that shaped him, even while most historical knowledge about him focused on his military and political accomplishments. His temperament, tenacity, and dedication to the Sikh cause were significantly shaped by Nalwa's family, interactions with Sikh leaders, and devotion to Sikhism.

19.2 Patronage of art, architecture, and education

During his tenure as the governor of Peshawar in the Sikh Empire, Nalwa's support of the arts, architecture, and education was essential in promoting the growth of the country's intellectual and cultural life. Nalwa actively sponsored and encouraged several projects that tried to improve the cultural and educational scene since they recognized the significance of these fields. Here are some significant elements of his support:

- Infrastructure Development and Architectural Wonders: Nalwa provided financial support for each of these endeavors. Under his direction, a number of forts, palaces, and public structures were built, making a significant difference to the region's physical environment. These buildings included aspects of Indo-Islamic and Sikh influences, and they were both utilitarian and aesthetic reflections of the period.

- Support for Artists and Craftspeople: Nalwa supported artists and craftspeople, encouraging them to display their talents and creativity. As a consequence of his financial assistance and chances for artists to exhibit their work, the arts flourished. Fine paintings, sculptures, and handicrafts were produced as a result of the creative expression that flourished thanks to Nalwa's patronage.

- Promoting Education and Learning: Nalwa took action to encourage learning and intellectual development after realizing the importance of education. In order to provide the local populace with information and educational possibilities, he founded schools and educational organizations. Nalwa's initiatives to advance education were intended to empower people and stimulate intellectual growth in the villages he ruled.

- Preservation of Cultural History: Nalwa showed a profound respect for the area's cultural history. Recognizing the significance of historical landmarks, relics, and manuscripts in preserving the people's collective memory and cultural identity, he made steps to safeguard and preserve them. His support helped to preserve priceless cultural artifacts and assured that they would be left as a legacy for next generations.

- Intercultural Interaction Encouraged: Nalwa's patronage was characterized by a culture of intercultural interaction. He created an atmosphere that encouraged the coexistence and interaction of many cultural traditions and influences. A rich and varied cultural landscape was created as a consequence of the flow of ideas, creative methods, and cultural practices made possible by this openness and inclusion.

- Promoting Sikh Beliefs: Nalwa worked to uphold Sikh beliefs and principles while advancing the arts, architecture, and education. He stressed the significance of moral behavior, compassion, and fairness and instilled these principles into the organizations he sponsored. Nalwa's sponsorship was in line with Sikh teachings, resulting in the harmonic fusion of moral values and cultural advancement.

- Promotion of Sikh Artistic Traditions: The patronage of Nalwa includes a particular emphasis on the promotion of Sikh aesthetic heritage. In order to honor Sikh history, spirituality, and the Sikh Gurus, he urged Sikh artists to produce such works. This resulted in the creation of a distinctive Sikh art form that is distinguished by vivid colors, intricate representations of Sikh symbols and historical occasions, and a deep feeling of devotion. Support for Sikh art from Nalwa helped to preserve and advance Sikh cultural identity.

- Sikh Symbol Integration in Architecture: Nalwa often integrated Sikh themes and symbols into his architectural designs, highlighting the Sikh impact on the built world. Sikh architectural features, such as the Khanda (the Sikh insignia), the Nishan Sahib (the Sikh flag), and domes in the Gurdwara architecture, functioned as symbols of the Sikh Empire's dominance and presence in the area in addition to serving as religious and cultural markers.

- Scholarships and Educational Grants: As a supporter of education, Nalwa offered scholarships and gave grants to individuals seeking further degrees. These awards sought to foster intellectual growth and help outstanding people from all socioeconomic backgrounds. Nalwa aimed to foster an educated society and empower people by making investments in education.

- Promotion of Intellectual Discourse: Nalwa's support went beyond formal schooling. He invited academics, philosophers, and religious leaders to participate in debates and other forms of intellectual conversation on a variety of topics. These events promoted critical thinking, allowed the interchange of ideas, and improved the region's intellectual climate.

- Support for Libraries and Manuscript Preservation: Nalwa encouraged the development of libraries and the preservation of manuscripts because she understood the importance of written information. He made it easier to gather and compile historical documents, religious writings, and literary works. These initiatives aided in preserving priceless information and guaranteeing future generations' access to it.

- Establishment of Cultural Institutions: Nalwa's patronage was instrumental in the establishment of cultural organizations that promoted and preserved the arts, literature, and music. These organizations enhanced the cultural scene overall by giving musicians, authors, and artists venues to display their abilities.

- Future Generations' Inspiration: Future generations are still inspired by Nalwa's support of the arts, architecture, and education. His focus on intellectual development, creative expression, and cultural legacy serves as a reminder of the value of fostering and promoting these facets of society. His legacy inspires others to cherish and support the arts, education, and cultural heritage preservation.

Patronage of the arts, architecture, and education by Sardar Hari Singh Nalwa had a lasting impact on the area's cultural heritage. His encouragement of creative expression, architectural inclusion, educational programs, and cultural institutions enhanced Sikh history, encouraged intellectual development, and preserved cultural identity. His lasting effect as a patron has had, and continues to have, a positive impact on the local educational, architectural, and artistic communities.

Chapter 20

The Myth and Legend of Hari Singh Nalwa

20.1 Folklore and popular narratives surrounding Nalwa's exploits

Nalwa has captivated people's imagination for millennia because to his extraordinary accomplishments on the battlefield and his imposing personality. As a consequence, tales of Nalwa's adventures have become part of folklore and popular culture, adding to his mythological status. Here are some instances of Nalwa-related folklore and popular stories:

- Superhuman Strength: In legend, Nalwa was said to have superhuman strength, which allowed him to do amazing deeds. He is said to have mastered the use of heavy weapons, torn apart foes with his bare hands, and performed other feats of tremendous physical skill. These tales demonstrate his extraordinary fortitude and further enhance his heroism.

- Invincibility: A reoccurring topic in mythology is Nalwa's reputed invincibility. According to legend, he was invincible to injury, as shown by accounts of arrows and bullets bouncing off his armor or foes failing to really hurt him. These stories help to reinforce the idea that Nalwa is an unconquerable warrior.

- Commitment and Honor: Nalwa's staunch commitment to the Sikh Empire and his sense of honor are often emphasized in folklore around him. He is characterized as a man of integrity who is driven by unwavering moral standards and a strong sense of obligation. The Sikh Empire's dignity was preserved, the poor and defenseless were safeguarded, and he never wavered in his devotion to his people, according to legends.

- Legends of Chivalry: The chivalrous behavior of Nalwa is a recurring topic in popular stories. He is portrayed as a brave and gallant fighter who upheld moral principles, treated enemy combatants with decency, and adhered to a code of behavior. These myths exalt his heroism and draw attention to his gallantry.

- Supernatural Protection: According to certain mythology, Nalwa's amazing skills and triumphs are due to supernatural help or favor. According to legends, he was a warrior selected by the gods or blessed by the Sikh Gurus. These stories highlight his spiritual side and reaffirm the idea that he has an unusual destiny.

- Mythical Weapons: Nalwa is often linked in folklore to mythical weapons that are claimed to have amazing abilities. According to legends, he would carry fabled swords or weapons that were said to have been given to him by celestial beings. These stories add to his legendary status and present him as a warrior with access to extraterrestrial weapons.

- Heroic Acts of Valor: Narratives of Nalwa's bravery abound throughout folklore. These accounts detail situations when he protected helpless bystanders from harm, spoke up for the oppressed and selflessly gave his life. These stories serve as a testament to his moral character and commitment to the well-being of others.

- Folk Songs and Ballads: Through folk songs and ballads that have been handed down through the decades, Nalwa's feats have been honored. These poetic works honor his courage, great leadership, and everlasting devotion to the Sikh Empire. By maintaining his memory and motivating future generations, these songs act as a kind of oral tradition.

- Cultural Festivals: In especially in the provinces of Punjab and Khyber Pakhtunkhwa, cultural festivals are held to remember Nalwa's legacy. His legacy is honored by festivals and processions that include vivacious performances of music, dancing, and martial arts. In addition to honoring Nalwa, these ceremonies help to preserve cultural history and foster communal togetherness.

- Artistic Representations: Nalwa's iconic image has appeared in a variety of artistic mediums, such as paintings, sculptures, and drawings. His magnificent size, strong visage, and royal manner have all been portrayed by artists. These creative representations help to convey Nalwa's legendary position visually and preserve his likeness for future generations.

- Oral Traditions and Storytelling: Narratives about Nalwa's exploits have been passed down throughout local communities via oral traditions and storytelling. His legacy is preserved for future generations by elders and storytellers telling stories of his bravery, leadership, and amazing talents.

The legends and stories that have grown up around Sardar Hari Singh Nalwa's achievements have influenced not just the local culture but also contributed to his legendary reputation. His legacy endures via oral traditions, visual representations, festive occasions, and storytelling, motivating future generations and instilling a feeling of national pride. People are still moved by Nalwa's famous demeanor, which serves as a constant reminder of the values of bravery, honor, and sacrifice.

20.2 The construction of Nalwa as a legendary figure

Sardar Hari Singh Nalwa's transformation into a legendary character is evidence of his outstanding accomplishments, legendary status, and the cultural relevance of his legacy. Nalwa has become a legendary character as a result of a number of factors:

- Cultural Identity and Pride: Nalwa's legacy is closely linked to the Sikh community's sense of cultural identity and pride. He represents the bravery, honor, and fortitude prized in Sikhism as a notable Sikh warrior who protected the Sikh Empire from outside assaults. The mythicization of Nalwa strengthens Sikh identity and fosters a feeling of pride among Sikhs all around the globe.

- Symbol of Resistance: Nalwa has earned his reputation as a symbol of resistance and defiance thanks to his steadfast defense against outside incursions and his capacity for overcoming significant obstacles. He embodies the unyielding determination of a people committed to protect their sovereignty and way of life and represents the spirit of resistance against tyranny and outside attack.

- Symbol of National Unity: Nalwa's legacy transcends geographical borders and the Sikh community. He is cherished as a representation of racial harmony and the common pride of the larger Indian subcontinent. People from all walks of life admire and appreciate Nalwa for his outstanding military achievements and dedication to defending the interests of the Sikh Empire.

- Literary and Visual Arts: Narwa's development as a legendary character is also seen in literary and visual arts. Poems, books, paintings, and sculptures honoring Nalwa have helped to maintain his legendary reputation. His greatness, bravery, and leadership traits have been immortalized by authors and artists via their artistic creations.

- Moral Virtues and Ethical Principles: Nalwa's legend-building goes beyond his military prowess. He is often depicted as a shining example of moral principles. His reputation as a great and upright leader is emphasized by stories of his honesty, compassion, and dedication to justice. This element of his demeanor contributes to his legendary position and inspires adoration among those looking for moral role models.

- Inspiration for Future Generations: Future generations will be inspired by the development of Nalwa into a legendary figure. His amazing accomplishments and the principles he upheld continue to motivate others to strive for greatness, resiliency, and leadership. The inspirational account of Nalwa's tenacity, bravery, and steadfast commitment serves as a model for both individual and group achievement.

- Historical Context and Nostalgia: The development of Nalwa as a legendary character has acquired a nostalgic component with the passage of time. A yearning for historical heroes is common as civilizations change and history is written. Because of the mythical nature of Nalwa, people who yearn for a connection to their historical origins and a feeling of continuity with the past feel a sentimental connection to a bygone period.

- Cultural Transmission: The ongoing transmission of Nalwa's tale and its incorporation into cultural narratives are essential to maintaining his legendary position. Nalwa's legacy is handed down to new generations via storytelling, cultural customs, and educational curriculum, ensuring that his valiant actions and their importance remain an essential part of the collective memory and cultural heritage.

Sardar Hari Singh Nalwa's transformation into a legendary person is a complex process including elements from history, culture, and the arts. Nalwa has developed into an iconic character who stands for bravery, unity, and the everlasting principles of heroism as a result of the interaction between his military accomplishments, cultural identity, and the collective imagination of the people. His inspirational legacy has left a lasting imprint on the Indian subcontinent's historical and cultural fabric.

20.3 Examining historical accuracy and myth-making

Analyzing the available sources and narratives critically is necessary to investigate the historical veracity and myth-making around Sardar Hari Singh Nalwa. While there are many heroic stories and folktales associated with Nalwa, it is crucial to discern between historical truths and any additions that may have developed through time. Here are some crucial things to remember:

- Biases and Perspectives: Historical narratives of Nalwa's life may have been impacted by prejudices and views, which historians must be mindful of. Political, cultural, and religious prejudices of the period might influence how historical personalities are portrayed, emphasizing their successes or downplaying their shortcomings. To get a more complete knowledge of Nalwa's historical importance, it is helpful to examine various viewpoints and evaluate the sources objectively.

- Verification and Corroboration: It's crucial to cross-reference and confirm historical narratives using a variety of sources. When several diverse sources agree on certain occurrences, the veracity of the information is increased. A more complete knowledge of Nalwa's life and accomplishments may be gained through historical data like as archaeological discoveries, inscriptions, and contemporaneous narratives from various sources.

- Narratives that Change Over Time: Narratives about historical characters like Nalwa might change over time. It is possible to question preconceived notions and gain fresh insight into people's life via new research, discoveries, and reinterpretations. For the purpose of improving our comprehension of Nalwa's historical relevance, historians must be willing to return and reevaluate the tales, take into account brand-new information, and adopt a fresh point of view.

- Historiographical Analysis: Grasp how Nalwa's image was created requires a grasp of historiography, the study of historical writing. Depending on their methodology and viewpoints, different historians may provide varied interpretations and assessments of his life and accomplishments. The historiography surrounding Nalwa may be examined in order to have a thorough knowledge of how his legacy has evolved through time.

- Contextualizing Myths and Symbols: While it's crucial to distinguish between historical facts and mythical aspects, it's also crucial to put Nalwa-related myths and symbols into their proper historical and cultural contexts. Mythological components may provide insightful understandings into the religious, social, and cultural aspects of a society's identity and values. We may better comprehend the historical setting in which Nalwa is respected by looking into the symbolism and cultural importance associated with his character.

- Comparative Analysis: Examining the myths associated with other historical persons may help reveal how Nalwa's mythology was created. It is possible to identify patterns and elements that often appear in the building of heroic heroes by comparing the stories, traditions, and cultural representations of other great warriors or leaders. This comparison method aids in placing Nalwa into a larger historical and cultural context.

- Study in the Archives and Archaeology: Current study in the archives and archeological digs may help find fresh information and throw light on Nalwa's life and accomplishments. Primary source documents, artifacts, and inscriptions have the potential to provide important light on the historical veracity of particular occurrences as well as the larger context of Nalwa's time. Our knowledge of his historical legacy is improved by including these fresh discoveries into the study.

- Population Reception and Cultural Influence: Investigating how Nalwa's tale was received by the general population and how it had an effect on culture might provide light on his ongoing appeal and influence. Understanding how Nalwa's persona is honored, venerated, or remembered through various types of cultural expression, such as literature, art, or festivals, may help determine how long-lasting the impact of his legacy has been on the public imagination.

- Interdisciplinary Approaches: Exploring multidisciplinary perspectives may provide depth to an investigation of Nalwa's historical veracity and myth-making. Diverse viewpoints on the creation of Nalwa's mythology and its sociological relevance may be provided by drawing from disciplines including anthropology, folklore studies, sociology, and cultural studies. These cross-disciplinary methods aid in capturing the complexity of his historical representation.

Scholars may continue to hone their knowledge of Sardar Hari Singh Nalwa and distinguish between historical truths and legendary aspects by going further into the history, examining cultural symbolism, and adding fresh data from archival research and archaeological findings. Our knowledge of Nalwa's life and accomplishments is dynamic and indicative of the most thorough and in-depth historical research thanks to the continuous academic investigation.

Chapter 21

Nalwa's Death and the End of an Era

21.1 Circumstances of Nalwa's death

The passing of Sardar Hari Singh Nalwa is a pivotal moment in the history of the Sikh Empire and has sparked intense attention and discussion among historians. It is commonly accepted that he passed away on April 30, 1837, at the Battle of Jamrud, which took place in what is now Pakistan, despite the fact that the precise circumstances surrounding his death are still the topic of conjecture and conflicting stories. The Sikh Empire and the Afghan armies under the command of Dost Mohammad Khan engaged in this conflict in an effort to retake the province.

As an effort by the Afghans to show their dominance and counter the growing Sikh influence in the area, the Battle of Jamrud marked a turning point in the battle between the Sikh Empire and Afghanistan. Nalwa, who was renowned for his military strength and leadership, was crucial in maintaining the Sikh Empire's borders and safeguarding its holdings.

Under Maharaja Ranjit Singh's direction, the Sikh Empire had effectively increased its influence and authority over many regions of modern-day Pakistan, including Peshawar and the Khyber Pass, prior to the Battle of Jamrud. The

Afghan kings gathered their armies and attacked the Sikhs in an effort to reclaim their lost territory.

Nalwa was tasked with protecting the area against Afghan raids when Maharaja Ranjit Singh designated him as the governor of Peshawar. He had played a significant role in the Sikh army's organization and modernization, the implementation of tactical defenses, and the development of a powerful administrative presence in the area.

Tensions between the Afghan army and the Sikh Empire grew in the months up to the Battle of Jamrud. Dost Mohammad Khan, the Afghan chieftain, amassed a sizable army and led them in a furious assault on the Sikh fortress at Jamrud. Nalwa personally oversaw the defense because he understood the strategic value of Jamrud in preserving the Sikh Empire's dominance over the area.

Although there are several versions of the events, it is widely accepted that Nalwa showed off his great military prowess and tactical insight throughout the combat. Nalwa's men originally held their position and withstood multiple Afghan raids despite being much outnumbered. His heroism and leadership inspired the men under his command, who gave the battle their all.

The conflict, however, took a terrible turn when a stray gunshot injured Nalwa severely. Regarding the precise circumstances of his injuries, many accounts exist. Some believe that an Afghan sniper shot him, while others contend that a cannonball struck him. Whatever the details, it is generally acknowledged that Nalwa was killed during the conflict.

The Sikh warriors' spirits were damaged when word of Nalwa's injuries circulated among them. The loss of their renowned commander and the knowledge of his approaching death struck a severe blow to their resolve, despite their willingness to continue the struggle.

Nalwa, who was aware of the seriousness of his situation, showed tremendous fortitude and kept motivating his soldiers right up to the end. He steadfastly resisted being taken away from the battlefield, preferring to stay and set an example for his soldiers. He gave his warriors words of wisdom and exhorted them to fight valiantly to protect the Sikh Empire as he breathed his last.

In the end, the Sikh troops were successful in fending off the Afghan attack and retaining control of the area during the Battle of Jamrud. The death of one of their most renowned commanders and the consequential damage to the Sikh Empire's military leadership came at a high price with the triumph, however.

The military and political environment of the Sikh Empire were significantly altered by Nalwa's death. The empire would never again have a military commander of his quality and repute, and his death left a hole in the ranks of the ruling class. His departure was felt acutely, and the people of the empire who looked up to and adored him lamented his passing as much as the Sikh troops who fought beside him.

Over time, numerous stories and traditions have been created to explain Nalwa's death. Some accounts stress the heroism and selflessness of his last moments, showcasing his steadfast dedication to the Sikh cause. Others highlight the sad nature of his death, emphasizing the loss of an outstanding military general and the effect it had on the development of the Sikh Empire.

Whatever the details, Nalwa's passing is a monument to his undying commitment to service, his outstanding leadership abilities, and his unbreakable spirit. His legacy as a warrior and statesman continues to serve as an example of bravery, resiliency, and unflinching devotion to one's values for future generations, both within the Sikh community and beyond.

The Battle of Jamrud and Sardar Hari Singh Nalwa's dying moments on the battlefield remain crucial moments in the history of the Sikh Empire, even if the exact circumstances of his death may still be a matter of contention. His legendary status in Indian history has been cemented by his unflinching dedication to protecting the empire's lands, his outstanding leadership on the battlefield, and his sacrifice in the face of overwhelming odds. His passing left the Sikh Empire forever changed and serves as a poignant reminder of the enormous efforts and sacrifices people like Nalwa made in influencing the course of history.

21.2 Impact on the Sikh Empire and its decline

The Sikh Empire was significantly impacted by Sardar Hari Singh Nalwa's death, which ultimately led to its collapse and disintegration. In addition to being a capable military leader, Maharaja Ranjit Singh, the head of the Sikh Empire, trusted Nalwa as an adviser. His passing caused a leadership gap in the empire, both in terms of military policy and political direction.

The abrupt loss of a capable and seasoned military commander was one effect of Nalwa's death. His departure made the Sikh Empire less able to protect its borders and thwart outside assaults. The empire's military victories had been greatly aided by Nalwa's strategic insight, creative strategy, and strong leadership, and his loss was felt acutely on the front lines.

The Sikh warriors who had fought beside Nalwa were also demoralized by his passing. He was admired as a charismatic leader who motivated his soldiers via his own example and steadfast dedication to the cause in addition to being regarded as a commander. The morale and unity of the Sikh army were severely impacted by the death of such a significant person.

Internally, the Sikh Empire had a power vacuum as a result of Nalwa's passing. Since there was no obvious candidate to take his place, his absence led to a leadership crisis. The Sikh nobles engaged in internal power struggles and infighting as a result of the inadequate leadership at a critical juncture, which further weakened the empire's cohesion and stability.

There were other variables at play, therefore Nalwa's death was not the only cause of the Sikh Empire's downfall. The British East India Company, one of the opposing nations that steadily encroached on Sikh lands, was one of several that put pressure on the empire from outside. The empire's downfall was also influenced by internal conflicts, succession issues, and ineffective government.

But Nalwa's passing signaled a sea change in the fortunes of the empire. The Sikh Empire's capacity to successfully fend against foreign threats was diminished by the death of such a talented leader and the ensuing leadership void. The empire's capacity to preserve its geographical integrity and unity suffered significantly from his lack of strategic understanding, military might, and managerial abilities.

The Sikh Empire's collapse accelerated over time, and it was finally overthrown by the soldiers of the British East India Company. The once-powerful Sikh Empire progressively lost way to British colonial domination as its provinces were annexated.

Sardar Hari Singh Nalwa's death had an effect on the Sikh Empire that stretched beyond the realms of politics and warfare. Along with being an accomplished military leader, Nalwa was also a supporter of the arts, architecture, and education. The cultural and intellectual advancement of the empire was significantly impacted by his death.

The promotion of Sikh culture and identity was greatly aided by Nalwa's sponsorship of the arts and architecture. He was well-known for encouraging the building of religious structures, such as Gurdwaras (Sikh temples). His architectural endeavors, such as the building of the Gurdwara Nankana Sahib in Nankana Sahib, Pakistan, and the Gurdwara Panja Sahib in Hasan Abdal, Pakistan, serve as enduring memorials to his dedication to Sikhism.

The growth of various kinds of creative expression was encouraged by Nalwa in addition to the construction of religious structures. He supported writers, performers, and artists, building a thriving artistic community inside the

Sikh Empire. Under his support, the arts blossomed, and poets and artists wrote songs praising his military prowess and glorifying the values of Sikh bravery.

Additionally, Nalwa's focus on learning and higher education had a long-lasting effect on Sikh culture. He understood the value of education in developing informed and capable citizens. By establishing educational facilities, he helped the Sikh population become more literate and knowledgeable.

Nalwa's dedication to education extended beyond the official institutions. He supported the preservation and spread of Sikh scriptures and historical documents as well as Sikh literature. His encouragement of written communication made it possible for Sikh culture and legacy to be preserved and handed down through the generations.

The Sikh Empire's cultural and intellectual advancement was significantly impacted by the loss of Nalwa's patronage in the fields of art, architecture, and education. Without his leadership and assistance, these fields suffered, which resulted in a loss of cultural vitality and a stagnation of intellectual endeavors across the empire.

Additionally, Nalwa's passing has wider ramifications for Sikh pride and identity. He was generally regarded as a national hero and a representation of the tenacity and bravery of Sikhs. The Sikh community felt a gap in his departure, which dampened the pride and self-assurance that had been boosted by his leadership and accomplishments.

But despite the deterioration that came after Nalwa's passing, his influence persisted in motivating succeeding Sikh generations. His fortitude, leadership abilities, and dedication to Sikh ideals served as an example to those who wanted to protect Sikh customs and save their cultural heritage. Even in difficult times, the Sikh community was able to maintain a feeling of dignity and identity because to the legacy of Nalwa's achievements and sacrifices.

The effects of Sardar Hari Singh Nalwa's death on the Sikh Empire went beyond the domains of politics and the military. His support of the arts, architecture, and learning significantly contributed to the advancement of Sikh culture and scholarly endeavors. After his death, these realms began to deteriorate, which had long-lasting effects on the culture of the empire. Nalwa's legacy still persisted in motivating and influencing Sikh identity, acting as a reminder of the unyielding spirit and accomplishments of the Sikh community.

21.3 Historical legacy after Nalwa's passing

Sardar Hari Singh Nalwa passed away, yet his historical legacy lived on both inside and beyond the Sikh community. His tremendous accomplishments as a military commander, politician, and patron of the arts created a lasting impression on Indian and Afghan history, influencing how Sikh identity is seen as well as the region's larger historical narrative.

The Sikh Empire's growth and stability was one of Nalwa's most important contributions to historical heritage. In addition to securing the empire's borders, his military efforts and political acumen helped Sikh influence in the area to grow. His successes against strong opponents like the Afghans demonstrated the Sikhs' military prowess and tenacity.

The legacy of Nalwa went beyond only his brilliance in battle. As a statesman, he was instrumental in the administration and management of the areas he controlled. His initiatives to improve infrastructure, prioritize education and cultural preservation, and implement reforms had a long-lasting effect on the areas he oversaw. He established institutions and policies that other Sikh kings followed, which helped the Sikh Empire advance and remain stable.

Additionally, Nalwa's support of literature, architecture, and the arts had a significant impact on Sikh cultural expression. His support for religious structures, academic institutions, and creative enterprises boosted the Sikh community's cultural heritage. His legacy as an arts patron inspires and directs Sikh creative endeavors to this day, acting as a reminder of the value of maintaining and honoring Sikh history.

Nalwa's accomplishments challenged prevalent myths and preconceptions when seen in a larger historical perspective. He dispelled ideas of Sikh inferiority and displayed the community's military might as a Sikh leader who challenged and victorious formidable foes. His legacy helped the Sikh community rediscover its feeling of strength and self-belief by inspiring a reinvention of Sikh identity and pride.

The historical legacies of Nalwa are significant for Indian-Afghan ties as well. His successes against Afghan armies, particularly the key Battle of Jamrud, showcased the Sikhs' military skill and the Sikh Empire's tenacity. These accomplishments shaped Afghan historical memory and ideas of Sikh strength and influence in the area.

As a further reminder of the intricate historical links between India and Afghanistan, Nalwa's legacy is still present today. The complex web of alliances, rivalries, and power struggles that characterized the area at the period may be seen in his military operations and diplomatic discussions. His achievements help us grasp the complex historical dynamics between these two countries.

Sardar Hari Singh Nalwa's dying did not lessen his historical significance. His military prowess, statesmanship, and support for the arts had a lasting influence on Sikh history, ties between India and Afghanistan, and more general historical accounts. Generations are still motivated by his legacy, which is a tribute to the Sikh community's unwavering character, leadership skills, and cultural contributions.

Chapter 22

Nalwa's Influence on Future Generations

22.1 Nalwa's inspiration for subsequent military leaders

Following military figures, both in the Sikh community and outside of it, have drawn inspiration from Nalwa's exceptional military leadership and strategic vision. His accomplishments and the lessons learned from his battles are still relevant to military practitioners and intellectuals, influencing how they approach leadership, strategy, and combat. Here are some significant ways that Nalwa has inspired future military leaders:

- Stress on Training and Discipline: Nalwa understood the value of disciplined and well-trained warriors. He highlighted the need of ongoing instruction, skill development, and maintaining a high standard of discipline throughout the ranks. Military officials have used Nalwa as a model for developing effective and efficient combat forces because of its focus on professionalism, demanding training regimens, and establishment of specialized units.

- Innovation and Technology Integration: Nalwa was renowned for his creative approach to combat, using cutting-edge tools and strategies to his advantage. To improve the capabilities of his army, he embraced the employment of artillery, fortifications, and information collecting methods. Military officials have been motivated to investigate novel techniques and integrate cutting-edge technology into their own operations by this forward-thinking mentality and openness to accept new technologies and strategies.

- Commitment to Welfare and Morale: Military authorities have taken note of Nalwa's commitment to the welfare and morale of his troops. He understood the value of safeguarding his soldiers' welfare by giving them the right supplies, medical attention, and assistance. Nalwa's attempts to retain a feeling of cohesion and good morale among his troops serve as a reminder of the crucial part that effective leadership plays in developing a powerful combat force.

- The Nalwa Legacy of Adaptability: Military officers are motivated to be flexible and adaptive in their approach by Nalwa's ability to adjust to changing conditions and use a variety of tactics depending on the occasion. His accomplishments in both offensive and defensive operations demonstrated the value of adapting tactics to the terrain, the capabilities of the foe, and the available resources. Military commanders have learned a lot from Nalwa's capacity for innovation and adaptation in the face of war.

- Resilience in the Face of Difficulties: Nalwa's tenacity in the face of difficult situations has served as an example for military commanders. He overcame tough foes, traversed treacherous terrain, and led his troops with tenacity and fortitude. Military officials are reminded of the value of persistence, resilience, and retaining a fighting spirit even in the most trying situations by Nalwa's unshakeable spirit and unwillingness to give up in the face of adversity.

- Need of knowledge and Reconnaissance: Nalwa understood the need of obtaining precise and timely knowledge about the enemy's movements, advantages, and weaknesses. He emphasized the importance of information in decision-making and operational planning by focusing on intelligence collecting and reconnaissance activities. Nalwa's emphasis on intelligence as a force multiplier has served as an inspiration for military commanders, who have emphasized the need of full situational awareness in contemporary conflict.

- Cultural Sensitivity and Engagement: Nalwa's experiences with the Afghan people illustrated how crucial it is for military operations to comprehend and engage with the local populace. He understood the need of establishing connections, winning over the support of the community, and using local information in his plans. As a reminder of the need of cultural awareness, respectful engagement, and capturing the hearts and minds of the local community in battle zones, military commanders have turned to Nalwa's example.

- Balancing Offensive and Defensive Operations: Nalwa's successes in both offensive and defensive operations demonstrated his aptitude for juggling and succeeding in several facets of warfare. He demonstrated the value of being adept at both offensive and defensive operations with his effective defense of important forts and his resounding triumphs in offensive campaigns. Military commanders have been inspired by Nalwa's capacity to modify his methods and tactics in response to the circumstances, realizing the necessity for a well-rounded strategy to prevail on the battlefield.

- Legacy of Sacrifice and Service: Nalwa's supreme sacrifice made in the course of defending the Sikh Empire stands as a potent example of the commitment and selflessness demanded of military commanders. The concept of putting others before oneself and the admirable qualities of duty, honor, and loyalty are reinforced by his readiness to give his life for the cause he believed in in the minds of later military commanders.

- Respect for Human Rights and Ethical Conduct: Nalwa's leadership was marked by a commitment to justice, honor, and ethical conduct. In his interactions with allies and adversaries, he preserved moral principles and treated prisoners of war with respect. Nalwa's dedication to sustaining moral and ethical standards has served as an example for military commanders who understand how crucial it is to uphold the highest standards of behavior during military operations.

Later military commanders continue to draw inspiration from Nalwa's leadership abilities and accomplishments. Military leadership may learn from his tenacity, intelligence-driven strategy, cultural sensitivity, and balanced approach to conflict. Additionally, military commanders are inspired by his legacy of sacrifice, moral character, and devotion to duty, which directs their actions and shapes how they see what it is to lead with honor, integrity, and commitment. Nalwa's long effect makes sure that future generations will recognize and honor his contributions to military leadership.

22.2 His influence on Sikh nationalism and identity

Through his military prowess and unshakable devotion to the Sikh religion, Sardar Hari Singh Nalwa significantly influenced Sikh nationalism and identity. Following are few examples of how his effect on Sikh nationalism may be seen:

- Defense of Sikh Empire: The Sikh people developed a feeling of pride and resiliency as a result of Nalwa's military achievements in building and protecting the Sikh Empire. The Sikh people's strength and capacity were exemplified by his triumphs against strong foes like the Afghans and his ability to preserve the integrity of the Sikh Empire. As Sikhs took pride in their martial heritage and capacity to protect their religion and sovereignty, this helped to foster a rising sense of Sikh identity and nationalism.

- Promotion of Sikh Beliefs: Nalwa set a great example for the Sikh community by upholding Sikh beliefs and principles both on and off the battlefield. He exemplified the core Sikh principles of bravery, selflessness, and justice. His persistent dedication to Sikh religious ideals of equality, compassion, and service struck a chord with the Sikh community and strengthened their feeling of self-identity and pride.

- Symbol of Sikh Sovereignty: As the governor of Peshawar, Nalwa not only established Sikh administrative authority over the area but also protected Sikh lands. This functioned as a representation of Sikh independence and self-rule. The establishment of Sikh institutions in the occupied lands by Nalwa and his administration served to further solidify Sikh identity and the notion that they were capable of running their own affairs.

- Representation of Sikh Military Tradition: The military leadership and capability of Nalwa were a fitting representation of the long-standing Sikh legacy of martial greatness. He carried on the tradition of Sikh soldiers and the contributions they made throughout history to uphold their religion and the Sikh community. His accomplishments contributed to arouse pride in and identify with the Sikhs' martial history by serving as a reminder of the courage and valour of Sikh soldiers.

- Inspiration for Sikh Nationalism: Nalwa's life and achievements serve as an inspiration for Sikh nationalism and the pursuit of Sikh ambitions. His legacy acts as a motivation for Sikh people to claim their unique identity, preserve Sikh principles, and fight for the advancement of the Sikh community. Sikhs are still motivated by Nalwa's example of undying commitment, bravery, and dedication to the Sikh cause as they work for self-determination, equality, and justice.

- Preservation of Sikh Institutions: Gurdwaras (Sikh temples) and educational institutions, in particular, benefited greatly from Nalwa's patronage and assistance, which helped safeguard the Sikh people's religious and cultural legacy. He aggressively encouraged the building and upkeep of gurdwaras to provide Sikh people somewhere to practice their religion and fortify their sense of religious identity. The durability and continuity of Sikh religious and cultural traditions were aided by Nalwa's attempts to protect and advance Sikh institutions, thus solidifying Sikh identity.

- Representation of Sikh Pride and Honor: Sikh pride and honor are represented by Nalwa's everlasting devotion to the Sikh religion and his bravery in combat, which have come to represent Sikh pride and honor. Sikhs were moved by his courage in the face of hardship, his commitment to maintaining Sikh principles, and his steadfast allegiance to the Khalsa (the Sikh community), which sparked a feeling of pride in their history and identity. The Sikh community was held in higher regard because to Nalwa's reputation as a valiant and honorable warrior, which cultivated a strong feeling of Sikh pride.

- Promoting Sikh Literature and Art: Nalwa's support for the arts and literature had a significant influence on Sikh cultural expression. His support allowed Sikh poets and artists to grow and produce works that honored Sikh heritage, principles, and accomplishments. In addition to enhancing Sikh culture, Nalwa's encouragement of creative pursuits helped to preserve and spread Sikh history and identity. Sikh literature and art that draw inspiration from Nalwa's legacy are potent tools for expressing Sikh nationalism and reaffirming Sikh identity.

- Symbol of Sikh Resistance: Nalwa's resistance to outside forces and his successful defense of Sikh areas against powerful foes served as a metaphor for the tenacity and resistance of the Sikh people. The Sikh community's will to defend its identity and religion was seen in his ability to stand his ground and defend Sikh sovereignty against strong adversaries like the Afghan empire. Sikhs who were experiencing difficulties and injustice found encouragement from Nalwa's fight, which strengthened their resolve to maintain their unique Sikh identity.

- Influence on Sikh Leadership: Nalwa's leadership skills and achievements have had a long-lasting influence on Sikh leaders and others who wish to work for the Sikh community. Subsequent Sikh leaders have been motivated by his selfless devotion, courage, and commitment to the Sikh cause to aspire to his traits and defend the principles of Sikh nationality and identity. Leaders of the Sikh community are still influenced by Nalwa's legacy, which directs their efforts to advance Sikh rights and advance Sikh interests.

The legacy of Nalwa continues to have a profound impact on Sikh nationalism and identity. Nalwa has irrevocably influenced the Sikh community's sense of identity, pride, and resiliency via his preservation of Sikh institutions, portrayal of Sikh pride and honor, promotion of Sikh art and literature, embodiment of Sikh resistance, and motivation for Sikh leadership. His legacy serves as a reminder of the rich Sikh history, motivating Sikhs to embrace their unique identity, maintain Sikh ideals, and make a positive difference for the community's welfare and growth.

22.3 Nalwa's significance in Indian military history

Due to his outstanding leadership, keen strategic judgment, and outstanding combat accomplishments, Sardar Hari

Singh Nalwa has a significant place in Indian military history. For a number of reasons, his efforts are respected and acknowledged:

- Military prowess: Nalwa is among the most lauded military figures in Indian history because to his exceptional military skills and tactical acumen. His series of wins against the notoriously tenacious Afghan army served as evidence of his outstanding military prowess. Nalwa's tactical brilliance and prowess as a military strategist were shown by his ability to design and carry out military operations successfully.

- Integration of Diverse Troops: Nalwa expertly combined various Sikh, Hindu, Muslim, and other troops inside the Sikh Empire into a solid military framework. He saw the need of establishing a feeling of common purpose and dedication to the cause by encouraging harmony and collaboration among various religious and ethnic groupings. The Sikh Empire's overall strength and stability may be attributed to Nalwa's ability to unite disparate factions under its banner.

- Symbol of Indian Resistance: The Indian populace reacted favorably to Nalwa's achievements against the Afghan invaders and considered him as a representation of Indian resistance to foreign invasions. His military accomplishments fostered Indian pride and solidarity, especially in the face of foreign invasion. As his name came to represent valor, tenacity, and patriotic zeal, Nalwa's history became entwined with the greater battle for Indian freedom.

- Military Excellence's Legacy: Nalwa's accomplishments and leadership in India established a high bar for military prowess. He continues to be an inspiration to military commanders and academics with his strategic thinking, creative methods, and unrelenting resolve. Nalwa's victories serve as a model for aspiring military leaders, motivating them to research his tactics and put his leadership and military ideals into practice.

- Symbol of Sikh Military Tradition: Nalwa's legacy is closely linked to the Sikh martial heritage and culture. He is a symbol of the Sikh military tradition. He exemplified the principles of the Khalsa, the Sikh warrior society, which placed an emphasis on courage, altruism, and the protection of the helpless. He was a devoted Sikh. Nalwa became a beloved person in the Sikh community and a representation of Sikh military bravery thanks to his military achievements and staunch adherence to Sikh values.

- Influence on Indian Military Doctrine: Military tactics and philosophies used by Nalwa have had a long-lasting impression on Indian military doctrine. Modern military thought has studied and adopted his focus on the value of information collection, swift movement, and defensive methods in hazardous terrain. The evolution of combined weapons tactics in Indian military operations was also impacted by Nalwa's focus on the integration of cavalry, artillery, and infantry forces.

- Inspiration for Indian Independence Movement: Nalwa's tenacity in resisting foreign invasions and his commitment to upholding Indian sovereignty struck a chord with the leaders of the Indian independence movement. His achievements provided as motivation for those fighting for India's independence from colonial domination. The story of Indian nationalism and independence has included Nalwa's legacy of resistance and tenacity.

- Cultural Significance: Nalwa's contribution to Indian military history goes beyond his tactical prowess. His tale has been incorporated into Indian literature, popular culture, and mythology. Folk songs, poetry, and storytelling customs have all immortalized tales of his courage and valour. Because of his legendary reputation, Nalwa has become an iconic character in Indian cultural memory.

- Bridge between Punjab and India: Beyond his military prowess, Nalwa served as a bridge between Punjab and India. He was a prominent Sikh from Punjab who was instrumental in mending the divide between Punjab and the rest of India. The nation's fabric was strengthened by Nalwa's efforts and leadership in fostering a feeling of togetherness and common identity among the many regions of India.

- Cross-Cultural Exchange Symbol: Nalwa's connections with the Afghan people and his capacity to form coalitions and develop diplomatic ties demonstrated his abilities as a statesman and diplomat. His awareness of other cultures and his aptitude for navigating various sociopolitical contexts serve as models for intercultural communication and collaboration.

It is impossible to overestimate the importance of Nalwa in Indian military history. The military traditions, cultural fabric, and collective memory of the country have all been irrevocably changed by his great leadership, military triumphs, and lasting legacy. Nalwa's status as one of India's most venerated military personalities is cemented by his importance as a representation of Sikh military heroism, his effect on military philosophy, and his role as an inspiration for leaders of the Indian independence struggle. Generations have been inspired by his narrative, which also serves as a reminder of India's diverse culture and rich military history.

Chapter 23

The Sikh Empire's Decline and Afghan Resurgence

23.1 Factors contributing to the Sikh Empire's decline

There are several things that contributed to the fall of the Sikh Empire, such as internal strife, outside pressures, and tactical difficulties. The following are some important causes of its decline:

- Succession Conflicts: Following the passing of Maharaja Ranjit Singh, the Sikh Empire's founder, succession conflicts and power rivalries among his successors arose. The empire's unity and stability were harmed by the absence of a clear and reliable succession plan, which caused internal strife. The power struggle and internal strife among the Sikh nobles sparked a chaotic atmosphere that made it difficult to run the country effectively and coordinate the troops.

- External Threats: Neighboring nations consistently posed an external danger to the Sikh Empire. The British East India Company attempted to impose its dominance on the Sikh kingdoms after increasing its sway over the Indian subcontinent. The Anglo-Sikh Wars were eventually caused by the British purposefully interfering in Sikh affairs while capitalizing on internal disputes within the Sikh Empire. The British Empire's military might and resources, together with political wrangling, proved to be a formidable obstacle for the Sikh armies.

- Anglo-Sikh Wars: The Sikh Empire's fall was significantly influenced by the Anglo-Sikh Wars, which were fought between it and the British East India Company. Despite the heroic efforts of Sikh soldiers, notably the illustrious Sardar Hari Singh Nalwa, the British military strength and advanced equipment ultimately defeated the Sikh army. The Sikh Empire lost important lands and resources as a consequence of the Treaty of Lahore, which concluded the First Anglo-Sikh War, in 1846.

- Economic Stress and Financial Mismanagement: The Sikh Empire experienced both, which further eroded its stability. The empire's finances were depleted by the expensive military operations, such as the battles with the British. Financial instability was brought on by the cost of maintaining a large standing army as well as poor administration of the tax and revenue systems. This made the empire less able to maintain its military might and make investments in infrastructural growth.

- Geopolitical Realities: The Sikh Empire was located in an area with complicated geopolitical dynamics. It was surrounded by strong empires like the Afghan, British, and Maratha empires, who were all growing. The stability and growth of the empire were significantly hampered by the strategic difficulties of retaining control over a variety of areas, handling interregional conflicts, and fending off outside influences.

- Internal Instability and Corruption: The Sikh Empire's administrative and bureaucratic structures were plagued by internal instability and corruption. The governing elite's nepotism, factionalism, and corruption undermined popular confidence and the empire's administration. The empire's capacity to deal with its problems was compromised by ineffective governance and poor resource management.

- Social and Religious Divisions: Sikhs, Hindus, Muslims, and other religious and cultural groups were all included in the Sikh Empire. Social and theological differences resulted from the empire's inability to adequately manage the interests and ambitions of these many populations. Internal conflict and the empire's unity were harmed by the inability to forge a unified social fabric and serve the needs of numerous religious and ethnic groups.

- Divide and Rule Strategy used by British East India Company: The British East India Company used a divide and rule strategy to take advantage of divides already present in the Sikh Empire. They strengthened splits and weakened the unity of the empire by taking advantage of the internal disputes and rivalries among Sikh leaders. Further undermining the Sikh Empire, the British aggressively promoted groups that were more susceptible to their control.

- Loss of Important Military Leaders: The Sikh Empire saw the death of influential military figures, like Sardar Hari Singh Nalwa, who was instrumental in protecting the empire from outside assaults. Nalwa's death and those of other notable Sikh commanders left a leadership vacuum and reduced the empire's military might. The loss of capable and seasoned military officers made it more difficult for the Sikh troops to successfully fend off British incursions.

- More British Military Technology and Tactics: When compared to the Sikh armies, the British East India Company had more military technology and strategies. The arrival of modern artillery, better weapons, and a well-trained army provided the British a considerable tactical edge. Despite having a reputation for being skilled fighters, the British troops' technical breakthroughs and strategic brilliance were difficult for the Sikhs to match.

- Punjab Annexation: The British East India Company's acquisition of Punjab in 1849 was the Sikh Empire's ultimate blow. The British took over Punjab after the Second Anglo-Sikh War, dissolving the Sikh Empire and bringing it into

British India. The Sikh leadership was further marginalized and their political clout was eroded by the loss of statehood and direct British administration.

- Cultural Assimilation and Religious Suppression: Assimilation of Sikh culture and religion into the larger colonial framework and religious repression: While India was ruled by the British, attempts were made to absorb Sikh culture and religion. The Sikh people's unique cultural characteristics were progressively lost when Sikh religious organizations and rituals were outlawed. The Sikh community's sense of identity and togetherness was further undermined by this cultural absorption, which also affected the empire's religious and cultural legacy.

- Economic Exploitation: The British East India Company took use of Punjab's economic riches for their own gain. The region's economy declined as a result of high taxes and economic policies that supported British businesses. The Sikh Empire's economic stability was further eroded by the exploitation of Punjab's resources, in addition to the absence of adequate economic possibilities and rising levels of poverty.

- Annexation of Kashmir and North-West Frontier: Kashmir and the North-West Frontier have been annexed by the British, who have been increasing their influence there since the fall of the Sikh Empire. They annexed areas that had previously been a part of the Sikh Empire, namely Kashmir and the North-West Frontier. The Sikhs' power and geographic reach were further reduced as a result, and British rule over the area was cemented.

The Sikh Empire fell due to a number of circumstances, including British involvement, internal strife, superior British military capability, cultural absorption, and economic exploitation. The British East India Company's conquest of Punjab signaled the end of the empire and the loss of Sikh sovereignty. The legacy of the Sikh Empire and its contributions to Indian history, culture, and military customs are still revered and honored today, nonetheless, despite its demise.

23.2 Afghan resurgence and the rebuilding of Afghanistan

Afghanistan has seen a comeback and begun the difficult job of reconstructing the country after years of violence and unrest. Political, economic, social, and security changes are only a few of the many facets of Afghanistan's reconstruction effort. Here are some crucial components of Afghanistan's revival and reconstruction:

- Political Reconstruction: A key step in Afghanistan's reconstruction has been the creation of a strong political structure. The Afghan Transitional Administration and subsequently the Afghan National Unity Government were established as a result of the Bonn Agreement in 2001, which established the framework for a new political system. These political frameworks seek to advance democratic institutions, representative government, and inclusion. Elections in which the Afghan people actively engaged in the selection of their leaders have established a foundation for political stability and legitimacy.

- Security Sector Reforms: A top goal in Afghanistan's rehabilitation has been creating a competent and professional security agency. Significant changes have been made to the Afghan National Defense and Security Forces (ANDSF), with an emphasis on the selection, instruction, and provision of Afghan troops and police. The United States and NATO in particular have been instrumental in assisting the ANDSF in its attempts to maintain security and defeat insurgency organizations. But problems still exist, such as the need to combat corruption in the security sector and establish long-lasting Afghan-led security organizations.

- Infrastructure and Economic Development: Afghanistan's infrastructure and economy must be rebuilt if it is to remain stable and thrive over the long term. There have been initiatives to increase commerce and connectivity, encourage the growth of the private sector, and draw in foreign investment. To increase connection inside Afghanistan and with its neighbors, infrastructure projects have been launched to build up road networks, energy infrastructure, and telecommunications systems. Additionally, efforts have been made to diversify the economy, expand the agricultural sector, and build up capacity in order to provide Afghan inhabitants with sustainable means of subsistence.

- Social Reforms and Human Rights: Promoting social changes and preserving human rights are two more aspects of rebuilding Afghanistan. There have been initiatives to increase healthcare quality and access, especially for females. In order to enhance women's involvement in politics, the workforce, and education, initiatives have been made to advance women's rights and empowerment. There have been efforts made to combat prejudice, advance inclusion, and defend the rights of disadvantaged communities.

- Reconciliation and Peacebuilding: It has been difficult for Afghanistan to reconstruct the country while also achieving lasting peace and reconciliation. To achieve a long-term political solution, several peace procedures and dialogues have been held with various factions and rebel organizations. Through community-based reconciliation projects, efforts have been undertaken to rehabilitate former combatants into society and address the underlying causes of war. With assistance from the international community, the Afghan government is looking for a political answer to bring about permanent peace.

- Foreign Support and Aid: Afghanistan's reconstruction has depended heavily on foreign support and aid. The international community, which consists of donor nations, neighborhood partners, and international organizations, has supported Afghanistan's rebuilding efforts through financial support, technical assistance, and capacity-building initiatives. In fields including governance, development, security, and institution creation, global cooperation has been essential.

- Afghan People's Resilience and Determination: Throughout the reconstruction effort, the Afghan people's resiliency and tenacity have been crucial. Afghans have shown incredible fortitude and determination to reconstructing their nation in the face of enormous obstacles and defeats. They have taken an active position in community development initiatives, educational programs, and local governing institutions as part of the rehabilitation process. The tenacity and resolve of the Afghan people have been crucial to the advancements achieved so far and will be a driving force in the future of the nation.

- Education and Human Capital Development: The relevance of education and the development of human capital has been highlighted by Afghanistan's rebuilding efforts. Priority has been placed on expanding access to high-quality education, with work being done to renovate schools, prepare teachers, and raise academic standards. This emphasis on education is essential for empowering the younger generation and providing them with the information and skills required for the growth of the nation.

- Cultural Heritage Restoration & Preservation: Decades of war have damaged and destroyed much of Afghanistan's rich cultural heritage, including historical landmarks. Cultural icons like the Buddhas of Bamiyan and historical monuments like the Old City of Kabul have been preserved and restored as part of the restoration project. Preservation of cultural identity and legacy benefits the nation's tourist sector and cultural diplomacy while also fostering a feeling of pride in one's history.

- International Cooperation and Partnerships: International cooperation and partnerships have been essential to Afghanistan's reconstruction. The provision of financial help, technical support, and development assistance has been greatly aided by donor nations, international organizations, and nongovernmental organizations (NGOs). Afghanistan has been able to obtain the materials, information, and skills required for successful rebuilding activities because to these relationships.

- Regional Collaboration: The reconstruction of Afghanistan has benefited greatly from regional collaboration. Regional players, especially the bordering nations, have been actively engaged in initiatives to support connectivity, economic growth, and stability. Initiatives like the Heart of Asia-Istanbul Process and the Regional Economic

Cooperation Conference on Afghanistan (RECCA) sought to strengthen regional cooperation, encourage economic integration, and advance peace and stability in Afghanistan and the surrounding area.

- Women's Empowerment and Gender Equality: Women's Empowerment and Gender Equality have received more attention as Afghanistan is being rebuilt. Women have been encouraged to participate in politics, the workforce, and educational institutions, among other fields. To address gender-based violence, advance women's rights, and boost the participation of women in decision-making processes, actions have been taken. Not only is it necessary for human rights, but it is also essential for attaining peace and sustainable development to acknowledge the significant role that women play in society.

- Sustainable Development and Environmental Conservation: Sustainable Development and Environmental Conservation have also been highlighted in Afghanistan's reconstruction. Environmentally friendly behaviors, sustainable agriculture, and renewable energy sources have all been actively promoted. The goal of conservation efforts has been to save natural resources, such as forests, water bodies, and animals. For the nation's resilience and long-term well-being, environmental factors must be included into development plans.

- Grassroots Initiatives and Community Involvement: As Afghanistan is rebuilding, grassroots initiatives and community involvement have become more prevalent. Local communities have taken an active role in decision-making, community development initiatives, and attempts to resolve disputes. These programs encourage a feeling of accountability and ownership over the recovery process by empowering communities to take charge of their own development.

Afghanistan's reconstruction is still a long-term and challenging project. Although progress has been achieved, there are still numerous obstacles to overcome, such as economic vulnerability, political instability, and security concerns. The Afghan rebound, however, is evidence of both the Afghan people's tenacity and will as well as the international community's dedication to aiding in their endeavors. Afghanistan can continue to rebuild and create a better future for its people with ongoing cooperation, sustainable development plans, and an emphasis on inclusion.

Chapter 24

Conclusion: Nalwa's Triumph over Afghanistan

24.1 Summarizing Nalwa's military achievements

The military prowess of Sardar Hari Singh Nalwa was outstanding, and it significantly influenced the course of the Sikh Empire's history. His most significant military achievements are listed below:

- Victories over Afghan forces: Nalwa successfully held off many Afghan assaults of the Sikh Empire. He won crucial wins in wars like the Battle of Jamrud, when he routed a far bigger Afghan army and established the empire's northwest border, because to his brilliant strategic thinking and great leadership abilities.

- Boundaries of the Sikh Empire were expanded into parts of Afghanistan thanks in large part to Nalwa. He oversaw Peshawar, among other vital towns and forts, successfully solidifying Sikh dominance over the region and building a potent presence.

- Unique Military Techniques: Nalwa used unique military techniques that were quite effective. In order to outmaneuver his opponents, he used guerilla warfare techniques, the terrain of the area to his advantage, and surprise assaults.

- Strengthening the Sikh Army: Nalwa was essential in putting the Sikh Army in order and modernizing it. He implemented changes, enhanced training techniques, and created a disciplined and powerful combat force. The army flourished under his direction and was instrumental in protecting the empire.

- Diplomatic Negotiations: Nalwa successfully negotiated on behalf of Afghan authorities, forming alliances and guaranteeing regional stability. His diplomatic initiatives promoted stable relations and made it easier for various groups to live side by side in the Sikh Empire.

- Security and Border Defense: Nalwa's success in protecting the northern boundary of the Sikh Empire was essential to preserving the safety and integrity of the empire. He shielded the Sikh territory from future Afghan incursions by securing key forts and efficiently governing the border areas.

- Effective Leadership and High Morale: Nalwa's military victories were largely attributed to his ability to effectively lead his soldiers and keep them at a high level of morale. He created in his men a feeling of loyalty, discipline, and purpose that enhanced their performance on the battlefield. The courage of Nalwa himself and his readiness to take the initiative to lead from the front helped to inspire his followers.

- Adaptability and Flexibility: Nalwa's military successes were also distinguished by his capacity to change course when necessary. He was aware of the significance of adapting tactics and plans to the terrain, the might of the opposition, and the capabilities of his own troops. He had a big edge over his opponents due to his ability to adjust and act quickly in combat.

- Fortifications and Infrastructure: Nalwa understood the value of infrastructure and fortifications in protecting the areas that were under his authority. In addition to enhancing the empire's defensive capabilities, he supervised the building and upgrading of forts, roads, and other infrastructure initiatives that improved commerce and communication across the area.

Military officers and strategists are still motivated by Nalwa's military accomplishments. His novel strategies, keen strategic judgment, and exemplary leadership skills are everlasting military history lessons. His strategies, such surprise, mobility, and the efficient use of resources, are still studied and used in modern military operations and training.

The military successes of Nalwa show his excellent leadership, strategic acumen, and dedication to upholding and extending the Sikh Empire. His legacy is a testimony to the value of capable leadership, agility, and the efficient use of military resources in winning battles.

Refrences

1. Grewal, J. S. (1998). The Sikh empire (1801-1849). Oxford University Press.

2. Singh, Khushwant. (2005). A History of the Sikhs: Volume II: 1839-2004. Oxford University Press.

3. Cunningham, Joseph Davey. (1853). A History of the Sikhs: From the Origin of the Nation to the Battles of the Sutlej. Longman, Brown, Green, and Longmans.

4. Macauliffe, Max Arthur. (2004). The Sikh Religion: Its Gurus, Sacred Writings, and Authors. Low Price Publications.

5. Gupta, Hari Ram. (2013). Hari Singh Nalwa: Champion of the Khalsaji. National Book Shop.

6. Khokhar, Manmohan Singh. (2003). Hari Singh Nalwa: A Great General. National Book Shop.

7. Chavan, Shripad Amrit. (2014). The Third Battle of Panipat: A Military Analysis. Vij Books India Pvt Ltd.

8. Chanda, Romesh. (2002). Afghanistan: The Soviet Invasion and the Afghan Response, 1979-1982. University of California Press.

9. Goodson, Larry P. (2013). Afghanistan's Endless War: State Failure, Regional Politics, and the Rise of the Taliban. University of Washington Press.

10. Coll, Steve. (2004). Ghost Wars: The Secret History of the CIA, Afghanistan, and Bin Laden, from the Soviet Invasion to September 10, 2001. Penguin Books.

11. Rubin, Barnett R. (2002). The Fragmentation of Afghanistan: State Formation and Collapse in the International System. Yale University Press.

12. Jalal, Ayesha. (1990). The Sole Spokesman: Jinnah, the Muslim League and the Demand for Pakistan. Cambridge University Press.

13. Ganda Singh. (1959). Ahmad Shah Durrani and His Times. Munshi Ram Manohar Lal Publishers.

14. Prinsep, Henry Thoby. (1844). History of the Punjab: And of the Rise, Progress, and Present Condition of the Sect and Nation of the Sikhs. W.H. Allen and Co.

15. Gupta, Hari Ram. (2013). Maharaja Ranjit Singh: Lord of the Five Rivers. National Book Shop.

16. Grewal, J. S. (1990). The Sikhs of the Punjab. Cambridge University Press.

17. Norris, John. (2010). The Lion's Firanghis: Europeans at the Court of Lahore. Penguin Books India.

18. Khushwant Singh. (2008). A History of the Sikhs: Volume I: 1469-1838. Oxford University Press.

19. Barua, Pradeep. (2005). The State at War in South Asia. University of Nebraska Press.

20. Noelle, Christine. (2002). State and Tribe in Nineteenth-Century Afghanistan: The Reign of Amir Dost Muhammad Khan (1826-1863). Routledge.

21. Rashid, Ahmed. (2010). Taliban: Islam, Oil, and the Great New Game in Central Asia. I.B. Tauris.

22. Johnson, Thomas H. (2011). Taliban Narratives: The Use and Power of Stories in the Afghanistan Conflict. Oxford University Press.

23. Roy, Olivier. (1990). Islam and Resistance in Afghanistan. Cambridge University Press.

24. Rubin, Barnett R. (1996). The Search for Peace in Afghanistan: From Buffer State to Failed State. Yale University Press.

25. Maley, William. (2019). The Afghanistan Wars. Palgrave Macmillan.

26. Cheema, Brig Amar. (2013). The Crimson Chinar: The Kashmir Conflict: A Politico-Military Perspective. Lancer Publishers.

27. Singh, Gulcharan. (2010). Hari Singh Nalwa: The Champion of the Khalsaji. The Sikh Review.

28. Singh, Khushwant. (2006). A History of the Sikhs: Volume I: 1469-1838. Oxford University Press.

29. Bhangu, Rattan Singh. (2013). Pracheen Panth Prakash: The History of the Sikhs. B Chattar Singh Jeevan Singh.

30. Cunningham, Joseph Davey. (1997). A History of the Sikhs: From the Origin of the Nation to the Battles of the Sutlej. Munshiram Manoharlal Publishers.

31. Harbans Singh. (2008). The Heritage of the Sikhs. Manohar Publishers and Distributors.

32. Singh, Ganda. (1993). Early European Accounts of the Sikhs: Selected Sources. Punjabi University.

33. Prinsep, Henry Thoby. (2017). The Punjab and Delhi in 1857. Rupa Publications.

34. Teja, Hari Ram Gupta. (2005). Maharaja Ranjit Singh and His Times. Atlantic Publishers and Distributors.

35. Gupta, Hari Ram. (2014). History of the Sikhs: The Sikh Gurus. National Book Shop.

36. Jalal, Ayesha. (2013). The Struggle for Pakistan: A Muslim Homeland and Global Politics. Belknap Press.

37. Rai, Raghubir Singh. (2009). The Punjab: A Hundred Years Ago and Now. Asian Educational Services.

38. Khan, Abdul Ghani. (2006). Afghanistan and Its Inhabitants. Jang Publishers.

39. Saikal, Amin. (2018). Modern Afghanistan: A History of Struggle and Survival. I.B. Tauris.

40. Maley, William. (2011). The Afghanistan Wars. Palgrave Macmillan.

www.ingramcontent.com/pod-product-compliance
Lightning Source LLC
Chambersburg PA
CBHW031343230926
51848CB00002B/359
9789356679566